Nadia's Heart

Part Two

Adventures in Evergreen Series

Wendy Altshuler

Library of Congress 938-341
ISBN-13: 978-1539729778
ISBN-10: 153972977X

Arborgate Media
For more information on the Evergreen Series,
visit http://arborgate.net.

A command rings out within me: "Dig! What do you see?"
"Men and birds, water and stones."
"Dig deeper! What do you see?"
"Ideas and dreams, fantasies and lightning flashes!"
"Dig deeper!"

"What do you see?"
"I see nothing! A mute Night, as thick as death. It must be
 death."
"Dig deeper!"
"Ah! I cannot penetrate the dark partition! I hear voices and
 weeping.
I hear the fluttering of wings on the other shore."
"Don't weep! Don't weep! They are not on the other shore.
The voices, the weeping, and the wings are your own heart."

—Nikos Kazantzakis

CONTENTS

CHAPTER I

NADIA'S HEART

This is the story of Nadia, who thought she had been born without a heart. She had a vague amnesia, and she did not know how she came to live at a cabin with an old man and an old woman. There were many things that Nadia did not know, or could not remember, but one thing was for certain: she felt that her heart was missing. She knew it to be true, but how was such a thing possible? She could not ask the old man or the old woman, or even the townspeople, because she felt she did not fit in, and that they would not understand. So, one night, Nadia uttered a wish to know about her heart, and a stranger with glowing eyes appeared in her room. His name was Georgeonus, and she set off on adventures with him in search of her heart and learned that her memory had been removed by an evil Voice from another land. But what they uncovered was an evil too horrible, too terrible to contemplate: this evil Voice had used dark magick to remove the tongues of the people of the Land of Silence, and now she was after children's hearts. But not just physical tongues and hearts—she removed the essence of those things for their power, through this dark magick. Now

Nadia and Georgeonus are determined to save the children's hearts from the Voice—before it is too late.

It was musty and damp. Always damp. This land had all the moisture and wet that the arid, dusty Land of Silence did not. She could not understand how the Books withstood all this moisture; there had to be a spell over them for them not to mold and rot in this place.

They had no chairs, only a table, upon which was spread whichever book they happened to have taken down from the walls of shelves—shelves all full of Books. They were ancient, historical books about the interjoining lands connected by Air Doors, interdimensional places on earth separated by these stationary passageways. There were no books devoted to magick and spells; these were special and had to be hunted down elsewhere. But there was information here, information on magick through historical accounts. For back when the books were written, magick was a commonplace wisdom. It was used by and for the people to live in harmony with the forces on earth, with those they had chosen to rule over the lands, and with each other. There was a checks and balances system for maintaining this order. It was an unspoken sense of harmony, and if things became imbalanced in any way, which was rare, the people could always trace it to someone whose actions were motivated by fear, or greed, or anger. Since the people had all that they needed, this hardly happened, and when it did, they gathered together to help whoever was the source of the problem.

But over time, evil had gained hold in the rulership of the lands, and the people were taught that the ancient magick was evil. They were disempowered and taught to depend on their leaders, who most often did not have their best interests at heart.

There were some who still knew of the old ways, who preserved the sacred wisdom and taught that it was more than legend. So now, as they pored through the books, they looked for the traces of magick and for clues to help them form a strategy to fight Talmus the Voice.

After an uncomfortable night of resting in shifts on the hard, splintered, wood floor, Nadia remembered that she had made strides, and she fought to keep her memory under control. They continued in their task of searching for a way to be rid of the Voice—for good. There must be a way, Nadia had thought initially, and so they searched through the magickal Books. When they started time again in the Land of Standhøfl Tourdemil, they needed something else to arm themselves against her power, something other than a lightning spell. If some creature or being was invisible, or using magick to become invisible, a lightning spell could make the person visible for a short time. There was a variety of lightning spells. Some harnessed its raw electric power, but many utilized its inherent magick to dissolve invisibility.

Perhaps Nadia's patience had begun to wear thin. She was tired not from the journey; not from the elements of heat, bitter cold, ice, and snow that she had endured; not from being suspected, captured, and abused by inhabitants foreign and unknown to her but from the constant unknowing of what she was doing here and why. She almost wished for the warmth of the old cabin house—her "home" as she knew it—its sounds and smells of dinner cooking, the old man and old woman whom she had grown accustomed to, and the knowledge of the comfort of sameness, so that when she awoke in the morning, all the simple things she was familiar with would be around her.

But now things were not certain. They were painful, patchy, and incomplete. The past was troubling, and she feared it was her own. She was remembering, but with that came realizations: that she was a part of this place, its history, its inhabitants. Inevitably tied.

She finally dozed off while sitting up against the protrusion of wooden shelves, which stuck into her back. She had been thinking that she wished she could awake from this horrible reality she now found herself in: of missing hearts and voices, of wars between peoples and forces she did not even know, of the inconvenience of the elements, and of the uncertainty of the success of their task. But she could not wake up from it, and the idea of sleep was appealing, so she let her eyes droop as her head settled down toward her chest.

The only thing that returning to Utsiket Sorghäven had done for Georgeonus was stir up memories—memories he would just soon forget. Wandering outdoors, he watched the waves in the distance and listened to the tide rolling onto the beach. It would be daybreak soon in Utsiket Sorghäven, and they had to devise some sort of plan. Based on the predawn temperature, it would be a warm, though not sunny day. In this land, one could only guess about a sun that lurked behind diffused clouds, offering a distant warmth. Here, the grey cloud cover never dispersed. Most, if not all the time, it was cool, damp, overcast, and raining. He hoped that during their visit, his special armor would not rust, although, having been here before, he knew this hope to be futile.

There was a dim sameness over this cloud-filled sky which made one question, day after day, if there even were a sun. It was not at all like his home, where the bright, quiet, arid atmosphere made most visitors shield their eyes. It was so foreign to him: the beach, the salt, the noise of the tide, the vast expanse of sea. Yet it was beautiful and cleansing. Unlike the fresh, pure spring in his own land, the ocean was natural, less contained, wild, and teeming with living creatures, a complex ecosystem of correlating alliances and adversaries.

There had been a question in his mind, and it kept repeating itself relentlessly. Sometimes, he felt as though he asked it aloud in the human language, though he knew that he did not. He merely directed his thought outward at the sea. If he were in his native land, where there were no audible voices—only thoughts—there might be someone to hear it.

Why had it happened? He thought all about those years that his parents had been exiled on an island here. He knew that a force had kept them there: a spell, or curse, devised by the Voice, for surely his father would have made a boat to return. A noble man was his father, the King, and it pained him much to see the helplessness on the King's face when Georgeonus had finally reached them. Seven years had been lost, and much more, to his parents, to the people of the Land of Silence, and to Georgeonus. But he was not thinking of himself now.

And as they pored over the Books, it troubled him more—a force, a spell, and a curse. But which spell it was, he could not tell, and this troubled him. For he knew most of them from the Books. Where had Talmus found the other spells? What magick did she know of beyond these Books that the lands possessed? Was such knowledge forbidden? If they had been armed with it, none of the poison of the Voice would have reached their land.

Something stirred in the cabin. Nadia was awake again. They had little time. He looked back at the dilapidated cabin, then at the immensity of the sea that surrounded the small island. What could they really find here? What magick? What hope did they have of ridding themselves of this evil once and for all?

What Georgeonus did not realize was that his thoughts were heard by someone rowing to them from across the sea.

As far as Georgeonus knew, Nadia's amnesia continued. There were moments, certainly, when her face betrayed some flash of memory or emotion, and now, in the hut, she had remembered the horrible day. Yet all of her memories about who she was had been eradicated by a spell from Talmus, so it was a surprise to Georgeonus that his face, and that of Holofernes, could trigger her mind out of a most powerful spell.

In earlier days, Georgeonus recalled, there were happier times in the Land of Silence. There were banquets, dinners, and celebrations, and an even tide of trade with the neighboring Standhøfl Tourdemil, which they reached through the magick of the Air Door at the Trees on the Hill. And, too, there was the arrival of a child in a basket at the castle.

How it had gotten over the moat and stood at the castle's front wall near the windows, he could not tell, but he was fascinated by the long, silver sword lain across its top. The elaborately carved sheath was protective and foreboding, and Georgeonus could not touch it, try as he might. His fingers were filled with shock, and then weakness, each time he came within an inch of its handle. A servant from the kitchen had come out to see where Georgeonus had gone, and finding him there with the basket, she summoned the Queen.

No one knew what the note in the child's blankets said (and the only one who could seem to remove the sword was the Queen). There were whisperings that the note was sealed by magick wax and addressed to the King and Queen. They were the only two who could handle the sword, which apparently also contained instructions.

Georgeonus would have liked to have had a playmate, although he generally entertained himself or enjoyed the company of adults. Those in the King's army took to instructing the boy in some sword fighting, even though the child had not formally begun his lessons. The girl in the basket was too young for companionship. After all, she was a baby, a girl, and not much fun to be around.

All seemed peaceful in the Land of Silence, until one day the servants and attendants of the court awoke to find that the King, the Queen, and Georgeonus had disappeared. Weeks later, Georgeonus was found near an Air Door, thought to be defective, called the Trees Above the Road. They were two trees suspended in mid-air, and little was known about whether the Air Door actually worked. Georgeonus was disheveled and holding an extremely large book. He was but four, and they soon learned, not alone.

The strange, terrifying, and powerful presence of the Voice began to be known and took over rulership of the land. Anyone who questioned her was instantly turned to a burning pile.

It was a most oppressing time. After Holofernes' accident or, rather, his battle with the Voice and the execution of a forbidden spell, Georgeonus found himself alone. He was alone as he had never known, unsure of what to hope for and how. He felt in his constitution a braveness and a knowledge that this situation was temporary: Holofernes' disappearance, the loss of his parents and his uncertainty as to whether or not they were still alive, the citizens who had been maimed and left to work the town's commerce without communication, those who had defected and fled through the Trees on the Hill, the newly granted power of some Metal-Wearer soldiers whom the Voice had dubbed her army, and her continuing oppressive and powerful force that she exerted over Georgeonus' spirit, trying to break him into devotion and servitude. Though her oppression seemed never ending and as if things were worsening, something protected Georgeonus from completely surrendering: some hidden, interior place that the Voice could never reach, of which she was always aware, and which she constantly attacked. Still, her powers weighed upon Georgeonus like a metal blanket. It drained his spirit, dimmed his vision and hope, and kept him confined mostly to the castle, especially in those first years. Later, he would venture out on errands for the Voice, as she tried to win him over by giving him more freedom. This did little good, as he could never, as prince, abandon his citizens to such tyranny, and he always returned.

When Georgeonus reached the age of ten, he felt that something in the kingdom was going to change. He was not sure what it was, but he had already begun searches beyond the kingdom for ways to get through the Trees in the Air—to find out what had become of his parents. Whenever Georgeonus passed the strange doorway, his eyes lingered upward as he devised ways of bypassing the invisible Door.

But it was not merely an Air Door. He remembered that there had been two. They were double doors, and Georgeonus had but one magical key.

The girl, Nadia, who years ago had been named and taken in by the King and Queen, had grown, and she somehow knew that in order not to create waves with the Voice, she had to be noticed as little as possible. She became a type of servant girl, fetching water, helping those cooking, cleaning, and sometimes assisting in the preparation of meals for the soldiers. Indeed, the Voice had expressed contempt when she did notice Nadia, but she had assumed that she was one of the servants' children. Nadia never spoke and hardly communicated, and so the Voice assumed that she was no threat and had been brought up in the Land of Silence without knowledge of her tongue.

The room that Nadia had been given by the King and Queen, full of fine clothes and furniture, was subsequently never used, as she slept always in the basement in her brown linen. She owned one blanket, that which had been in her basket, which she stored under a loose stone in the floor.

Nadia herself was unsure of her origin or role, and she only functioned as she had always done: out of pure instinct. It occasionally pained her to watch Georgeonus ascend the stairs heavily, being summoned by the Voice. She would remain leaning on one of the stone railings, gazing upward, watching the light on the silver metal, and wondering why the Voice lived there if she made everyone so crazy and unhappy.

She made a mental note to ask Georgeonus the same, and one day, as she was in the basement of the castle and noticed Georgeonus outside, she did.

But Georgeonus would not answer—he was uncomfortable, shrugging her question, saying he did not know, and disturbed that she should be asking such a thing at all, with the Voice around. Nadia persisted, but Georgeonus was gone.

The next time Nadia asked Georgeonus, he became angry, and when he began to reply, the Voice called for him. He shushed Nadia and walked away.

Nadia was hurt, but even more disturbed, by Georgeonus' behavior. And so she began to ask the kitchen folk and even some Metal-Wearers what the Voice was doing there if she was making everyone unhappy. Most of them just walked away from Nadia quickly. Others gave her a look of warning or alarm before doing so.

Nadia ventured out into the town to find out the answer to her newly escalating question. For the more she inquired, the more it became clear to her by the reactions (or lack of reactions) of the townspeople that the Voice did not belong there.

And then, as Nadia was sending a new inquiry to some factory workers, she was seized on both sides by two Metal-Wearer soldiers.

Fighting all the way up the road and stirring up fine dust, she coughed and kicked, trying to deter the Metal-Wearers in their stride. She was but seven, and promptly brought before an erected chair in the master bedroom on the third floor of the castle. The room felt colder than usual, and tense. As she stared into the chair she had a sinking feeling in her chest, as if she was about to be swallowed through the floors and into the earth. When the Voice spoke, the feeling got stronger. She could feel the Voice's power, and felt fear at what it was capable of—of killing her in a variety of ways.

I don't know what it is about you, but I knew I should have been rid of you from the start. There was a pause, a strange delay, and suddenly a spit of fire over Nadia's head. She ducked, holding her head, was met with silence and then another poof of fire on her other side, near her ear. She thought she heard a word of question uttered by the Voice. The Voice somehow seemed confounded, as if it were possible that Nadia might be protected from her destruction.

All right. Where is my Silver Commander? Georgeonus was in the room. He had watched anxiously as Nadia was brought up the stairs, feeling partially responsible toward his parents for not having answered Nadia's dangerous questions. He considered this, but stepped forward, as the Voice continued.

You're going away, dear—far away. And not to worry about all your troublesome thoughts. Within the next few hours, they will have vanished from your troublesome mind. Thoughts of you, of me, of this place, all will be gone, and in its place will be only the simple servant role you assumed. I banish you from this Land—you simple, meddling child—never to return again.

And at that, Nadia was seized again by the soldiers. Georgeonus had come up close to the chair to receive instruction from the Voice. He nodded his head and took a plain silver sword that was handed to him. Then he took out a silver key of his own, showed it to the Voice, and stepped away from the chair. Nadia was released by the soldiers, and Georgeonus grasped her right arm.

As they traveled down the road, Georgeonus would not speak to Nadia. She was infuriated by what she perceived to be stupefied apathy on his part—he, who was the prince! For she could tell, as of late, that he *was* a prince, though he was not really acting like one responsible for his kingdom. She shrugged his grip, which became tighter, and then a dark feeling began to come upon her in waves.

It was oppressive, like that when she stood before the chair: a sinking feeling inside and all around, which made her fear that she would be swallowed by the earth—and, too, the feeling that her mind was being pushed around, so that bits of her own memory and thoughts were sent far away, and she found her mind desperately chasing after them, like one trying to recall a dream, but more frantic, as if those thoughts contained the remnants of her very self. Georgeonus noticed that something was amiss within her as they walked along the road, then soared across the caramel-colored floor on his boots. But no sooner had she been seized by the episode than she was gradually herself again.

When they reached the Trees in the Air, Georgeonus stood absently below them, as if also under the influence of the Voice.

He looked at the key, not offering any thoughts to Nadia. And suddenly, Nadia grabbed it and ran back toward the hill.

She had a head start, for Georgeonus was still frozen, but he soon followed her. Nadia, an above-average swift runner, made it a good chase, continuing all the way to the birch Trees on the Hill. On the verge of a vague and nervous laughter, she opened it with the key, smiling, having seen the Metal-Wearers do so before, counting seconds as Georgeonus headed for her. He realized he could have easily caught her, since he was just as swift, and quicker in the boots, but his face revealed a mounting sadness that she had never seen before. She felt full of a new and wonderful, though painful, emotion, watching him approach. It was a happiness, to be with him, away from the castle, and a sadness at his state. She realized that she wanted nothing more in the world than to make his grief go away.

They left green grass behind. When Nadia passed through the Door, she knew Georgeonus followed, and she was delighted to no longer have the status of prisoner, at least not for the moment. They walked along cold ice, leaving the birch trees behind in the middle of a frozen lake and then ran, laughing, slipping toward the iceberg opening of the underground. They left the maddening silence of the Land of Silence and heard the sounds of their voices mingled in the air in full volume, dancing with gusts of audible wind that joined in. They rounded the iceberg mound and entered into a cavern that descended into warmth, and steam.

Again the sinking enveloped her. Nadia grabbed hold of a spike and raised one hand to her forehead in confusion. It was happening again, as it had on the road. All of the unpleasant memories of her childhood at the castle, and even the more recent ones with Georgeonus, were being sent away—pushed—out of her mind. She bent toward the cave floor, holding her stomach in fear as if she could contain the memories, viewing the warm rock and puddles, trying to record her surroundings. Peripherally she could see Georgeonus' boot as he came toward her. She wondered where she was, the sound of steam was confusing and foreign, but after a minute she rose, suddenly herself again.

It was not long when they again began to run, laughing. It became a game, though they knew not who was chasing who. It was just pure laughter and fun such that they had not known or been allowed to know. They continued through bogs of falling frogs, reaching hysteria as the creatures landed and twined through Nadia's hair and around posts. Their eyes rolled as they tumbled off Georgeonus' metal, and Nadia and Georgeonus both did imitations of their droopy expressions, turning, tilting, and falling as their delighted laughter echoed out to the canyon. At one point, they were spotted by a child of the Linen-Wearers, escapees from the Land of Silence who now dwelt in this underground. But Nadia and Georgeonus, too blissful in this newfound state of laughter, laughed at them too, and continued on, out of the caves and down into the canyon.

When their laughter had calmed, they walked, still smiling, catching their breath. They climbed downward, unsure of where they headed, and they didn't really care. And for the first time, they spoke, taking in the sense of real sound. They realized what the people in the Land of Silence had lost when their communication with each other had been completely taken away, even though they never spoke out loud before Talmus had arrived.

"Why do you stay in that castle? When the Voice makes everyone so miserable," asked Nadia. It was more a statement than a question. "Why don't you come here and live like the Linen-Wearers, and be free?"

Georgeonus stared thoughtfully at his boots.

"Where were you taking me, anyway?" continued Nadia. "Everyone knows those Trees in the Air don't work."

Oh but they do. I know they do. I've been through them.

Even though they were out of the Land of Silence, and there was sound here, Georgeonus' voice still had a metallic tone.

"You have? To where?"

To another Land. Georgeonus paused. *Besides, the Voice gave me the coordinates for a Door.*

"What Door? To where?"

To a Land I have not been to.

"What is it called?"

Man's Land.

"Man's Land," repeated Nadia.

It was so liberating, to be able to speak and act freely, without the Voice's oppressive presence. Nadia laughed, and

Georgeonus laughed too. They stopped and then burst out laughing again.

"Have you thought of going there to live?"

Where?

"Have you thought of going to Man's Land to live, instead of the Land of Silence?"

No.

"Why not?"

How could I have time to think of that, when I've only learned of its existence today? Besides, I could never leave the Land of Silence. It's my land—I've a duty to stay there. As long as the Voice is still there, I cannot leave. And. . .

"And?"

Georgeonus faced Nadia.

And I've got to find out what has become of my parents.

Nadia stared at her steps, for she knew now that they were the King and Queen, and that it was no accident that the Voice was in the Land of Silence. It all made sense.

They made it down to the lower levels of the canyon and continued to walk. They headed toward an area set back afar, which emitted a warm, yellow glow.

Suddenly again Nadia was seized with the oppressive amnesia—this episode so strong that she stopped and sat and stared at the ground, confused about where she was. She was not sure that whatever had hold of her would pass.

But when she did have a bearing on herself again, she realized that she was under a spell of the Voice. Georgeonus saw it happening too, and Nadia schemed for a solution.

"Georgeonus," she said as they were trying to decide what to do, "I am going to lose my memory. But I want to help you. There must be a way we can find your parents— and Holofernes too. I feel like I'm going to slip away soon— will you hold my hand?" Georgeonus joined his hand to hers and watched Nadia with a solicitous look. She felt a tear brimming and then running down her cheek; she felt that soon she would no longer be herself, and it was the most frightening feeling. He was her only friend. They had grown up together in the castle, and only recently had she come to know him. She cried out of her own fear, for she did not understand where she was going, what would become of her, if she had any control, or if she would ever return. But she cried mostly for Georgeonus, worried about how he might manage without her. Yet, he was the prince. How could she assume that he had any need for her, an orphan left at the castle in a basket?

Georgeonus sat by, holding her hand.

"I'm so glad we were able to come here, to talk and laugh, even if it were only for a small time. It has meant more to me than anything, and I want so much to help you…I—" But again the oppressive feeling seized hold, spreading forgetfulness through her mind. Her grip on Georgeonus' hand tightened, and she hunched over, as if her thoughts could be stopped from falling out. Then her hand became limp. This time the episode lingered, and she sat catatonic—a stilled creature.

Up until this time, Georgeonus had been going along under the oppression of the Voice. But Nadia had taught him to question, to not stand for things as they were. He had always felt that somehow she would help him eventually defeat the Voice. What would he do now without her? Georgeonus squeezed her hand and then slapped it lightly, feeling the beginning of Nadia's slipping away.

When Nadia came to, it was as though she were coming up for air for the last time. She squeezed Georgeonus' hand again, and her eyes filled with tears. She put her arms around the metal shoulders as tears dripped down the silver-armored back. She clutched the sleek metal, and Georgeonus' hand reached and patted her shoulder. He had had a very regal upbringing and was not used to such modes of expression.

Then, in an instant, Nadia realized that there was another, deeper layer of memory hidden within her that had nothing to do with the Voice's spell pushing itself upon her.

She saw in a flash—like the flashes of important memories of people about to die—that she had another existence that she did not remember: the existence of the child in the basket before it had arrived at the castle.

She realized that she most definitely had been delivered there to help them, and there was yet a deeper magick that they could use. Georgeonus knew all the forbidden spells from the Book of Spells. But there was a Force, a powerful Presence, more powerful than the Voice, more powerful than anything, and Nadia knew about it. The tears stopped flowing, and Nadia sat up and took a breath.

Nadia knew there was a spell that they could use to counteract this memory spell. She did not know how she knew, but the information had just come to her just when she needed it. She uttered a sentence, and she could hardly tell where it had come from. It was contained in her moment of struggle for survival. It had been delivered to her from within—from a place that was veiled to her now but which she was determined to uncover someday. It was contained in a deeper memory of a place that Nadia was only vaguely aware of—the place that she had come from.

"Promise me something," Nadia said, wiping her face.

Georgeonus did not move. She spoke calmly, and was hardly aware of the words when they exited her mouth.

"Take out my heart."

Georgeonus' head tilted to one side in questioning. She shook his arm, now convinced. She knew that this would be the last of her consciousness, and she had no idea that was what she was going to ask, or why, but the words came out of her mouth like instinct: a solution from a hidden source.

"Don't you see? If you don't do it, I might never come back. I don't know how I know it, but I do. It's the only way to counteract this spell. If I forget, and if my heart's in that forgetting person, I'll never be the same again. You can counteract her. You can save a part of me. You've *got* to save me so that I can come back. Please don't let her own me. Georgeonus! There's no time! Please! Promise it!"

As he watched Nadia's pleading stare, he tried to utter the words. He very well did know how to remove the essence of a heart, only because he had spent days decoding the most secret of spells, at the urging of the Voice—but how could he actually, humanly, do such a thing? What would happen? At the same time he felt that he must, and the words came forth, if only to appease her, as he whispered.

I promise.

Georgeonus felt that he was on the edge of a supernatural occurrence of some sort, and his mind kept returning, momentarily, to the child in the basket. He was disconcerted by the way in which Nadia had spoken, because she had conviction, as if this was meant to be. He suddenly rallied and then stood up, pacing, trying to remember the spell. He turned—no, that's not it, as Nadia braced the rock. Then he remembered.

He stood before her, suddenly stilled, as it came to him. His hands clasped together as if protecting a baby bird, and Nadia looked up. He felt the spell lurking, creeping in the distance like a dark shadowy entity. He came closer to her, his hands in front of her ribcage. He whispered, trying not to quiver, foreign words of power, as he gazed into the cave-like structure of his hands.

And it was done. They had heard the sound of wings flapping somewhere, and no sooner had it been done that the emotion and color began to leave Nadia's face, until she sat, as before, catatonic on the rock. But not from the loss of her heart. It was her memory. Nadia's face was blank, and her mind only attuned to the present. Inside her seemed a hollowed space.

Boom-boom. Boom-boom. Boom-boom.

Pumping in Georgeonus' wet hands was the warm, precious, beating flesh of a muscled heart. He held it, astonished, the sticky texture bonding to his palms and fingers. His eyes watered in the shock—though he had the character of a prince, he was but ten, and this was unlike anything he had ever seen or felt: a precious round heart held within his very hands, beating. He tried to know what to do, where to put it, and where to go. Nadia merely stood there absently and followed the nuances of his movement as he stepped, hesitating with the precious object. She followed as he headed gingerly on the canyon floor toward the yellowish cavern, to the constant sound of the heart's pump.

Georgeonus felt led by a supernatural pull. He followed it, hoping Nadia too would follow, which she did. He could not think of taking a hand from the steadily beating organ, warm and alive, for fear that it would stop and something truly disastrous would happen. They continued on for what must have been ten minutes. Georgeonus could not even fly, so careful was he in his steps with attention on the heart. And then, Nadia sat on a rock as if she were in a trance, and Georgeonus continued on, not worried about her escaping.

For his attention was on the approaching glow of the cavern. The path narrowed, and rocks on his path decreased as he walked on softer, flatter ground. The echoes of the canyon, of his steps, faded. It became so quiet, and there was a warm glow about. But it was not like the quiet in the Land of Silence: it was different. He had been near this part of the canyon before with a Wizard and the Wizard's brother, long ago, and Georgeonus could not remember when, or why, but it was as if he was being led here all along. The sole sound of the heart continued, and he looked down. His boots were on a lighter sand, lit by a warm glow like sunlight, and he stopped.

He sensed a Presence around him, and he had the knowing sensation that his parents, wherever they were, were still alive. He stayed there in the warm glow, experiencing a thankfulness if such a thing could be true, knowing it was, and hearing only the muffled beating that itself had quieted, as if in deference to a Presence all around.

And then, a stocky little creature was coming toward him. He thought it was a cave creature, but it was not. It had the bearing of some type of worker, with a purpose, and as it approached, Georgeonus saw that he was only about two feet tall. The servant began to open the buckle of Georgeonus' boots and then his metal, which Georgeonus stepped out of. He stood there barefooted in his linen on the fine, warm, cream-colored sand, the organ beating constantly in his hands.

Something called to him—it came from inside? It was gentle, yet commanding. He dared not delay, and he walked forward toward an even warmer, quieter, more peaceful glow. It seemed that what Georgeonus thought was quiet just paces ago and what he knew of quiet in the Land of Silence were all noise compared to this completely soundless Presence that cared so much for him, for his person. Now Georgeonus knew that he was definitely here to leave the heart, and he walked attentively, obediently, and a little frightened, toward that task.

He could hear some flapping noises on either side: two more servant creatures were flying toward him. They were stout, funny-looking creatures, like little dwarves with large noses, and their brown wings and large hands were more than half their own size. They approached to take the heart. There was no question that it was in no better care than here, with this Presence. They took it away and disappeared into the glow, leaving Georgeonus with bloodied, sticky hands. And although Georgeonus did not understand all that was happening now, or in the past, something assured him that it was all right, and that in the future everything would be complete.

When Georgeonus returned back some paces to the semi-warm and quiet place, the creature who had helped him out of his metal stood there presenting to him a hot, steaming cloth—a white terrycloth cotton—held up high on a stick, with which to wipe his hands. Georgeonus took it, and as he wiped he saw the blood soaked into it, the remains absorbed, and every last trace going from his hands. The more he wiped, the cleaner the cloth also became so that it was white again. It was scented and very clean, and his hands were completely sanitized and dry. He returned the cloth to a flying creature idling by, who held it by a stick and disappeared.

When Georgeonus returned to Nadia he knew what he had to do.

He led her, compliant as she was, back through the lands. With this disposition, and without her memory, she was docile, even slow moving. Georgeonus knew now that he had to get the sword. The sword had been hidden in the cleft of a rock in the basement by a servant, under the direction of Georgeonus' parents. It was his sword. Somehow he knew that the sword was his, though the time had never been right. But now it was time for him to get it, and he was going to have to figure a way to get out of the Land of Silence, as a duty to his people, to find his parents, wherever they were.

But first he had to get Nadia out of this place, and he was not going to leave her with the defected Linen-Wearers, for he could not tell where they might go. Besides, he had been given the coordinates to a new Door, with a time change, and permission to open it. He wanted to see what was on the other side, and he could not but help wonder that his parents might be there.

But where could he leave her? He could not just drop Nadia at someone's doorstep, and expect her to stay…

Could he?

It all seemed so perfect—too perfect: the old man and woman on the hill. When Georgeonus and Nadia arrived through the Door, they entered a forest, and not far ahead was a town. It was commerce as usual, apparently, for the busy townsfolk, but when each laid eyes on the boy soldier in metal, and the girl in worn-out linen, stares and whisperings ensued. By now Nadia was so complacent as to appear right at home—content in this new place, and whether the cause was the loss of her heart, or memory, or both, Georgeonus could not tell. They continued to walk through the town. Georgeonus saw no sign of his parents, but he was determined to scout out the surrounding landscape. He could faintly sense the Voice warning him, for they had been gone a time. Yet she knew that he would inevitably return, as did he, if not for the sake of duty alone.

CHAPTER II

HOLOFERNES' RETURN

No one who saw Holofernes rowing would know of his affliction. None could determine it, unless they saw his face. Even though Holofernes had lost his sight, he had gained powers of discernment never before known to him. All of his senses had become heightened. It was rare that he got into trouble at finding his way, for he had explored adjoining worlds countless times.

He headed determinedly toward the island, always eager for scent, for sound, and for other things. Things which Georgeonus was not yet aware. Thoughts. Questions. They had spoken so much in earlier years, in the silence of their land, through thought. Their thoughts were always their own, harbored, until directed at another. But this did not seem to apply in other lands as easily as in the Land of Silence. Perhaps it was the dryness of the air which allowed the thoughts to pass more quickly; perhaps it was the close vicinity by which they stood to one another; or perhaps it was a combination of properties of the land itself, which they were not aware of. Yet now, years later, in the dense thick of this waterlogged, misty place, Holofernes listened. And every rare, silvery sound that came fighting through the air: faint, but slicing, caused him to shift his oar, this way and then that. He knew it would be only a matter of time before the rear of the boat happened upon the small shore.

Georgeonus and Nadia had been over and over their options until the day slipped into afternoon. Predictably, the overcast sky turned to rolling clouds and soon rain. Even though time was on their side, they must act, for they did not yet understand the consequences of what had been done. Time stood still, but at what cost?

There was a knock at the door.

When Georgeonus opened it, he was met with the sound of the pelting rain, and the sight of a majestic suit of gold armor confronting his own silver metal suit. Although they had searched for Holofernes, Georgeonus had not realized that he was hardly prepared to confront him. But now here he stood, hair drenched, his tan body smeared with mud in places, the golden curls of his hair worn down by dirt, dust, and mist.

The three remained: Holofernes at the door, his blackened eyes communicating to Georgeonus, who held the door handle, confronting his childhood caretaker and captain of the King's army. Nadia sat on the floor, only more troubled by this presence from the past. With Georgeonus and Holofernes together, it made her uneasy feelings even stronger.

As Holofernes stepped into the hut, it appeared that he and Georgeonus were already involved in a silent, thought-transmitted conversation, the contents of which Nadia could only imagine.

As she observed Holofernes' face, she had the same vague memories as those that overtook her in Georgeonus' presence. Like Georgeonus' blinding white eyes, the black hollow voids of Holofernes' conveyed emotion and expression. They revealed great turmoil and guilt, and he seemed to apologize to Georgeonus, whose quiet only impelled more turmoil. Suddenly there was a piece of parchment in his hands. Nadia recognized it, and she shot a look up at the blackened sockets of the soldier. The emotion of memory teased her and pierced her heart— wherever her heart was—and she imagined the pain to it like the ghost pain of a severed limb. Holofernes gestured to Georgeonus with the parchment. She recognized it as the Lightning spell from that day at the castle—the spell that Holofernes had used to save Georgeonus, and with which he had doomed his own sight.

Georgeonus and Holofernes walked out onto the beach, and were there for a time, heatedly talking and pacing. Nadia stepped out onto the sand, feeling it between her toes, and watched a bright haze rising from the horizon, still unable to break through the mist. She felt the warmth of the new day and warmth in the knowledge of being in the presence of friends with whom she had a history. But could they trust him? Holofernes had been under the influence of the Voice. Finally they walked toward the hut, resolved to their task at hand. Holofernes looked at Nadia with a trace of acknowledgment.

Once inside the hut, Georgeonus brought Holofernes up to speed on the time spell. But Holofernes, after hearing Georgeonus out, was more concerned about having a strategy before starting time again in Standhøfl Tourdemil. Georgeonus listened to Holofernes, and he considered as Holofernes sketched out some possible proposed plans with the few things that were lying on the table.

You are going to need an army that is prepared—prepared to act the second that time starts. There won't be any time to explain to them what the strategy is. They've got to be readied to strike.

How? asked Georgeonus.

We arm them. We arm them and strike when time begins.

There was really no gathering of their things, no stopping to plan anything else. Before Nadia could tell, they were out the door and rushing back for the Air Door. In fact Nadia felt that she was trying to keep up as Holofernes and Georgeonus continued their talk through long, swift strides down the beach, half in and half out of earshot of what she could hear.

Nadia shouted after them, "But what are we going to do after that? What about a spell to counteract the Voice? We can't just start a war and expect her to go away!"

They turned to notice Nadia yelling, standing on the beach.

We have no spell. And we cannot leave time stilled without incurring repercussions from the Ruler Unseen, answered Georgeonus.

"Well, if you don't mind, they're my repercussions to worry about. I'm the one who stopped it."

What then do you propose? asked Georgeonus.

"I don't know. But we need magick, or knowledge of magick. There must be somewhere we can go for that."

We will go to see the Wizard of Hill Country, said Holofernes. *But we cannot leave time stilled any longer. The punishment will affect all of us.*

When they had landed at the Trees in the Sand to go back into the Land of Silence to gather weapons, Nadia lingered behind. She stood with her arms folded, kicking small stones on the beach and mumbling to herself.

"Why should we trust him?" said Nadia, half to herself, half to Georgeonus. "It could be a trap. I saw him through the ring, setting up the machines, and then again, unlocking the cell doors where the children were being kept."

"Ah. But you did not see what happened after that," whispered a voice in Nadia's ear.

"Prince Talman?" She smiled.

"Holofernes let the children out, all right," he said. "He was trying to save them. A few of them got away, but they were so confused by the cold, they went back to the others. He was going to release the men, and I think he was planning on leaving Standhøfl Tourdemil, but a guard saw one of the children and called the squad."

"But what snapped him out of the Voice's spell?"

"That I don't know."

"Then what happened?"

"The rest you saw in the ring. Holofernes must have escaped and gone back to the Land of Silence. He went through the Air Door, that I know. But the children…"

"We stopped it in time. Right?"

"I'm afraid not. Not all of them."

Prince Talman thought back to what he had seen in the ring.

An instrument moved toward a boy's chest, and he was strapped into the chair by it. It was square, with clamps and cold steel angles. A contraption lowered from its top: a flat metal plate with a round, wrought-iron black cage seated on it, which had pointed, jagged ends bent toward its center. A thick glass vial with a leather strap around it dropped down into the cage. Then the entire configuration positioned itself in front of the boy's chest. Something inside the machine began to whir and spin as a cold light was emitted from the cracks along its side. A lamp suddenly illuminated a round circle on the left side of his chest, exposing his heart within, which lay beating at a quickened pace. Those watching marveled as the light began a pulsing which imitated the heart, dimming and brightening to the heart's rhythm. Suddenly the light intensified, and in the concentrated glare those nearby watched shapes form in the circle of cold light, like shadowy fingers moving within it. Flapping sounds of fluttering wings whisked above them, and the boy's eyes widened. Some in the hall ducked—they thought a bird had entered and was flailing itself against the walls. But there was nothing above them. The working whirred feverishly to a high pitch, the boy squirmed and heaved quick, interrupted gasps, and suddenly the red, beating organ, cut off at the valves, lay contained in the glass container. The workings slowed, and the machine dimmed.

But the boy continued to gasp suctioned breaths.

"The lever, you fool!" said the Voice with impatient scorn as the boy's gasps became high-pitched gulps. A guard ran to the machine and lifted a lever on the left, and the machine sounds whirred downward, slowly through the gears of its mechanics. A round soldered ball came down in front: two cold metal semicircles wrought together by pins and bolts. It came to rest, finally, in front of the boy's chest as he collapsed and convulsed. It clunked into place and slowly opened, revealing a rough grey stone seated inside. Again the machine began to whir. They boy was now stilled in the chair. The engine roared faster and faster, lighting up the boy's chest, and faster than anyone could see the stone was pelted out, and the boy sat up with a startled expression, and the machine's whirring winded down. His expression soon dulled.

Then the heart in the container disappeared, and reappeared in one of the glass cases on the walls.

"Prince Talman?" called Nadia, bringing Prince Talman back to the beach.

"Let's just say you didn't save them all," he answered. "Some of them got *processed.*"

Georgeonus called for Nadia.

"Prince Talman, come with us," said Nadia, running toward the Trees in the Sand. Then she asked, rather reluctantly, "How many?"

"Twelve."

CHAPTER III
FIGHTING BACK

When they start time again in the Land of Standhøfl Tourdemil, the men would be armed.

They had retrieved a spell from the Book that Georgeonus had for starting time again. It was not so much a secret spell that was hard to find, or one that no one could access, but one which carried a warning of retribution. So the question was more whether one should venture the risk to use it.

Back in Standhøfl Tourdemil, Holofernes and Georgeonus reached the bottom castle floor and began to arm the men with axes, bows and arrows, spiked sledge hammers, and clubs, which they unloaded from a sleigh they brought into the hall. They also gathered the children at the end of the hall to assemble with Nadia, who would load them into the sleighs outside. They were like maintenance workers in some bizarre stage show, positioning and moving the statue-like figures in their frozen postures as Georgeonus readied the spell.

Under his direction, Nadia had placed a bowl with the red powder in it on a pedestal. Georgeonus sprinkled the potion they had prepared onto it and read magick words. The liquid consumed the powder in a fizzle, and a blast of red smoke emerged out of it into a swelling cloud. Then, there was a deep rumble in the earth, and the ground shook. As if some huge unseen cogs beneath the earth had been set into motion, the floor underneath them lurched, jerking everything forward as if the entire earth turned on its axis. Forward they lunged, catching themselves, and suddenly there was movement around them. Then there was confusion and mayhem in the hall. All the men knew was that they were suddenly freed from the cells and armed. They yelled and charged the stairs in unison. Upstairs, the guards saw that the children were gone, and that they were being ambushed. Holofernes wasted no time in engaging in battle with any Eskimo, anywhere. He combated with skill unsurpassed by the lot, soon leaving scattered men in his wake.

Nadia gathered the startled children and told them to go wait out at the sleighs. She could not help but be troubled by those who responded sluggishly and simply vacantly stared as they were ushered along by others.

There was so much chaos—what with time starting abruptly to the utter amazement of all who had been frozen asleep—that it was minutes before the Voice caught on.

"Stop this! Stop this!" Nadia heard the Voice scream. But the guards were outnumbered and outweaponed.

Nadia, Georgeonus, and Holofernes knew that Voice could burn them, so Georgeonus lifted his sword toward the ceiling, conjuring a lightning bolt. Storm clouds formed, and a bolt shot down, which he caught with his sword and sent toward the chair. Many ducked from the shuddering boom that caused all to cower and cover their heads. This did not include Talmus, now a giant, visible woman dressed in a silk robe, with long black flowing hair. She stood up tall from the chair and gained her full height, surprising Nadia by how tall she actually was. Talmus seemed unfazed by her visibility and walked straight for Georgeonus. Nadia made a motion toward her, and without looking, Talmus lifted a palm, which sent a shock of force, sending Nadia flying against a wall. The Voice lifted the other palm toward Georgeonus, who blocked a vicious current with his lifted sword as he slid toward her, his boots sliding along the floor. Their movements were familiar, almost a greeting, like two who had fought in a confrontation before.

Screaming children ran about. Nadia recovered from the high fall, and clutching her rib, she reassembled the children and pushed them toward the front door.

But then, the ground rumbled and the building shook. All stopped fighting, paused, and then started again. Minutes passed. The Linen-Wearers were winning the battle. Talmus had gotten closer to Georgeonus and was closing in on him. Again, the ground rumbled, this time sending them all off their feet.

It was an earthquake. The building began to crumble around them.

Talmus disappeared. The guards ran to the back of the castle, to what exit the Linen-Wearers did not know, and the Linen-Wearers headed to the front of the building. Other Linen-Wearers noticed Holofernes and Georgeonus jump onto the sleigh and joined them. But there were no dogs. How were they to pull it? The sleigh lifted into the air to reveal what had been fashioned on its bottom: tiny whirring wheels.

The sled surged forward as bits of ceiling crumbled and cascaded down. Nadia and the children had reached the entranceway and were running down the stairway.

"Into the sleighs, quickly!" she shouted. She hoped the men would get out safely. As they jumped into the sleighs, the mountain shifted and cracked underneath them. The children screamed in panic.

"Stay where you are!" shouted Nadia as she ran to the front of the sleigh and grabbed the reigns. She noticed that the dogs, who had become wolf-like and transformed in their journey up the mountain, had returned to normal. They squealed and barked with alarm and had already begun to pull the sleigh to escape.

Out of the castle doorway, came running men and then Holofernes and Georgeonus flying on the sleigh, with more shouting men behind them. Nadia cracked the whip as one man grabbed the reigns of the other sleigh, and men jumped onto the back of it. They headed for the road, away from the castle tumbling toward them, hoping the mountain itself would hold until they could get to the bottom. But what awaited them at the bottom was a sheet of ice, and it too could crack and send them down into the frigid deep.

She had never driven a sleigh nor a team of dogs before. The pure instinct of survival now taught her. As they rounded the rough road, more slippery now as they gathered speed, their path looked grim. Giant chunks of the castle came descending down, hitting the mountain's jagged sides and causing avalanches of huge falling debris. The children screamed, and Nadia wanted to do the same and take refuge closer in toward the mountain, but there was nothing that would shelter them. She kept focused on the dogs in front of her, thinking only of getting to the bottom. Cascading from above came another rock, and the children held onto the sleighs, terrified. Nadia tried to turn the sleigh toward the mountain to avoid it. They swerved dangerously around the edge of the road.

Something also descended from the sky. It was a black figure, but Nadia could not even think about another potential threat as the second sleigh bore down upon them, rushing behind her. They swerved back to a straight course, barely missing the rolling boulder which crashed onto the road.

The second sleigh had to stop to clear it. When Nadia looked back, Holofernes and Georgeonus were flying behind the teams, and they stopped to help the other sleigh as the impending black figure approached Nadia.

Flapping folds of heavy black fabric enclosed the figure approaching them as it flew and dipped up and down in the wind. It was heavily cloaked, and Nadia could not see a face. She was also still driving the sleigh, so had only glanced back, but then the figure came up alongside them.

Now the whole mountain began to shake and break apart from rumblings beneath. Nadia stopped the sleigh in a panic. The ground underneath them cracked, and the crack travelled down the road and ahead, splitting it open wide. They would be swallowed up into it if they continued. Looking back, she saw in an instant that the men in the other sleigh rushed to climb onto Holofernes' and Georgeonus' team, and all the while the mountain crumbled. Nadia lost her sense of reality as her senses were overloaded and adrenalin coursed through her.

Above, shadows of sections of the cliff began to fall down upon them.

The black figure was beside them. As the boulders fell, the figure unfurled what Nadia could only discern as a quilt. It suddenly surrounded their sleigh and enclosed them, and pulled them away from the mountain.

The rocks and sections of mountain coming down upon them did land on the quilt, but bounced off buoyantly. Still they were jostled about, and as they flew inside the quilt, they could see and hear the dark shadows—bouncing, then smashing. The dogs whined and looked above, or sat low, nervously unsure of the magick enclosing them. The children were silent, looking around as they sat in the shadowy enclosure of the white quilted cloth. All grew quiet as they continued to fly.

They continued this way for miles until it became clear that they were descending. The temperature then changed;

they must have entered the underground. Soon, they landed. Everything stopped. And suddenly the cloth opened up.

They were in the canyon, and Georgeonus and Holofernes were not far behind. Georgeonus flew alongside the overloaded sleigh, boosting its power with his wheels to lift the additional weight.

The cloaked figure had hold of the quilt. The black fabric covered its head and most of its face, but Nadia could see that the skin surrounding its eyes was silver. It looked directly into Nadia's eyes. The dogs and sleigh lay on the quilt, but the figure pulled it out instantly like a tablecloth trick, flapped it up in the air and then jumped up onto it. It held onto the edges and flew away, glancing back to stare once more at Nadia.

Mothers came out of the cave, and some children and mothers ran into each other's arms, rejoicing and crying. The other sleigh landed, and there were more grateful reunions. It was fortunate that the earthquake had not done damage to the underground.

"What happened? Did you destroy Talmus?" asked one of the mothers holding her child.

"No," said Jasper, "we only got out just in time."

"Where's Richard?" asked Jasper's wife, Jennie Jervinis, looking around frantically.

The mothers quickly realized that several of the children, who had been processed by the machine, were not okay.

"What's wrong, James?" asked one mother holding her son's chin and the back of his head as he stared off into the caves.

Their blank faces were cold. And even though their eyes were membranes, they were like greyed glass on a rainy day. The children were docile, unfeeling, and slow moving. They walked with fragile steps, as if they could not see. The children did not speak, and when spoken to, it was as though they were trying to remember who they were, what they had been looking for, or what the name was of the person speaking to them. A stone sat within them, and coursing through their veins was a stark, gritty substance. How this mystery was accomplished, through magick, no one could tell.

The inevitable had happened: that which they thought they could prevent through sheer heroic effort. Blindly they thought that goodness would prevail. They did not believe in the horrible possibility: Nadia, Georgeonus, Holofernes, the people of the Land of Silence. Because they had come from one in their past, and all sufferings that had happened since seemed mild.

Until now. For now it was all happening again, and these were *hearts*. What would it mean?

Nadia was surprised to see the number of Linen Wearers emerging from the caves of the underground. As word spread, they came in greater numbers and came still. Many of the Linen Wearers did not speak, and Nadia suspected that she knew the reason.

"There must be a way to stop this Voice, once and for all," said Jasper to Georgeonus and to all of the other Linen Wearers within earshot. "What of magick? What of the hidden realms and the other lands? It is high time we utilized that knowledge to fight back!"

"You cannot fight her. We cannot even see her," said one woman.

"I say we go see that Wizard of yours," one man said to Georgeonus. "The one who was rumored to have helped the King and Queen. Where is he?"

"Yes, how do we find him?" said another, as more urgent voices joined in.

"He must know something!"

Georgeonus stepped up on a large rock and raised his hand. His silver suit shone even in this dim canyon, and it contrasted against the earthen hues and the dirt-laden rags of the people.

"There is such a Wizard. And I shall go to see him, to see what might be done. But please, know that we have exhausted many spells. Talmus the Voice is a creation of the Ruler Unseen. He is the higher authority."

"We must appeal to him, then. Tell the Wizard that something must be done. We need aid!"

Georgeonus jumped down to confer with Jasper as many in the crowd argued amongst themselves. Some suddenly quieted down, and the quiet spread as they noticed something in the distance.

Shapes were moving toward them, and all turned to see, for they thought that all of the Linen Wearers had already gathered. It soon became apparent that they were not Linen Wearers, but a species that was part giant, reaching an average of nine feet tall. They moved at a brisk pace, and there was something recognizable on the shoulders of one of them. It was Richard, riding like a monkey on the shoulders of a woman giantess warrior. The rest were men, dressed like fishermen, but equipped with weapons, belted with knives and swords. Nadia bristled when she recognized Tars in the front—the man who had kidnapped her and Richard.

When his mother saw Richard, she advanced, and then she hesitated. But her instincts were strong, and she ran toward him with her arms outstretched. He happily embraced her and ambled down from the height as the woman giantess joined the rest of the men.

There were traces of remembering on the faces of both the giants and the Linen Wearers as they stood facing each other, a silent gap between them save for Richard and his mother. For long ago, trade had flourished between the lands, before the Trees above the Road had been sealed. Now, they stood face to face, and the anger from the defectors of the Land of Silence was palpable and apparent.

"It is your land that has poisoned us with Talmus the Voice," said one Linen-Wearer. "Your Trees Above the Road have brought this calamity upon us!"

A man beside Tars stepped forward. He resembled Tars, but he looked younger, and his hair was blond.

"Our lands are joined," he said. "You cannot separate yourselves from the lands connected by the Doors. All knowledge, all legends, all magick, and all rulers apply to all the lands. It is the ancient way."

"This disease—this *evil*—has come from your land," said another. "Our people—our *children*—have been mutilated by this Voice! It is you who have to make this right!"

"We have come to offer assistance in fighting Talmus the Voice. We cannot fight her alone," the man answered.

"Then what is to be done about her?" asked an elder Linen-Wearer. "Talmus cannot be destroyed."

"It is not what must be done about her. It is what is to be done about yourselves," said the woman giant.

"What in the world does that mean? How did you come through here?" asked another Linen-Wearer. "There is no Door in the underground, connecting our land to yours."

"We have been given passage by King Talman," answered the giantess. "He has watched the recent—event— and called an assembly. We are here to aid you."

"And why should we trust all of you?" asked Nadia, staring directly at the man Tars. "What do you have to gain by helping us? What's in it for kidnappers and brutes?"

Watching the exchange, the blond man answered, "We keep a close eye on the Trees in the Sand, and what comes through there. I am Lars, and my brother Tarsimun is a guardian of the door. We know things about the Voices that you do not, since they originate from our land. You have lost many of your legends. We know what Talmus has done, and we want to set it right. And," the man paused, searching for the right words, "our waters are rising because of this imbalance. Soon we will have to retreat to the underground, when there are no islands left."

An old Linen-Wearer spoke up. "But that is a legend. You cannot believe that the waters truly are the tears of the Ruler Unseen."

Some of the Linen-Wearers were processing information they had never heard before. There was no answer from the giants.

"We will deal with Talmus later," Georgeonus said. "First we must save these children's hearts, while they still can be saved."

"He is right," said Holofernes. "There is still time to reverse the spell. We mustn't delay."

"Tell you what," said Jasper in his booming, jolly voice, putting a protective hand on Richard's head. He faced Georgeonus, Holofernes, and Nadia. "Why don't you all hurry along and find the Wizard, and we will entertain our guests in the meantime. To find out exactly what it is they have in mind."

"We have three days," Georgeonus said, jumping down from the rock and joining Holofernes and Nadia.

CHAPTER IV
THE SILVER WITCH

Holofernes knew where to find the Wizard as of late, although not just anyone could visit the Wizard at any time. It had to be an important matter involving the welfare of a lot of people. Besides that, his castle moved around a bit. And so, Nadia, Georgeonus, and Holofernes headed back to the Land of Silence and were traveling up the gravel road when something happened. Only, they did not know what had happened until moments later.

They remembered that her visit had been preceded by a magick dust.

The dust came from above, the air tingled, and miniscule, silver particles glistened as they fell. It was musical, and as they breathed, they smelled fresh air like new spring, and they felt an excitement of imminent magick. She appeared suddenly, and at first no one knew where she had come from or how; she was just there on the road. She came as naturally as if she had approached them from the road. But as the magick dust settled, they realized—remembered—that the Silver Witch had dropped out of the sky.

As she stood there smiling at them, they remembered that they had looked up at the sky at a circling dot which descended. As it approached, it formed the shape of a square, floating quilt. The Witch was soon revealed to be sitting on top in black garb and hat, her silvery skin thick and rubbery. With both hands placed on diagonal corners of the quilt, she jumped off and shook the fabric out like clean laundry and parachuted down to them, the tennis sneakers on her feet ready for the road. Softly she landed, snapping the quilt upward and folding it once, twice, three times, and again and again until it was a small square deposited into one of her pockets.

No one had thought to look out for the Witch, and this was useless, since her arrival was always unpredictable. The Silver Witch never came particularly from the west, or the east, or the north or south, so one could never quite tell where to watch out for her. She did not always come when visitors were in dire need of her services; she just showed up at random times, although later the wisdom of her visit could always be discerned.

The Silver Witch was dressed in layers of a black robe, the layers under the arms cut for freer movement. It seemed unsuitable for the dry, bright climate of the Land of Silence. Her hat was high and pointed, but most astonishing were her face and hands. They were the only skin visible, and they were coated in silver. Her flesh was soft and moist, and the wrinkles in her smiling, middle-aged face were coated with the thick substance, giving it a shiny, rubbery appearance. Smelling like the freshest spring air, she approached Nadia and said her name, and then kissed half her lips and half her cheek, as if unable to decide between the two and unable to resist either. This she did to the others, calling first their names and then bestowing upon them the special kiss. It was like a blessing from one who not only carried great power and knowledge and who could be a great ally, but also one who was inclined to talk straight to you like a friend and tell you the truth when you needed to hear it—yet it would be somehow bearable, never painful when it was delivered by her voice.

Nadia remained stunned on the road in the bright glare, and her lips and cheek turned silver to reveal the encounter: a silvery, gooey sheen which made her skin partially metallic, like the Witch's. As the minutes passed, the glistening substance dried and became powdery, escaping from her skin as sparkling particles drifted into the air.

Who is that? wondered Nadia, after a moment.

I don't know ~ answered Georgeonus.

The Silver Witch left this goo on everything that she touched. There was something vaguely comforting in her rubbery chin beneath that smile—a physical ugliness that was betrayed by an inner beauty beyond her form and an internal goodness that shone brightly. There was something about her that made you want to be near her. It was not because she was pretty; in fact, she was rather mannish: big, with round shoulders, a soft middle, grounded, square feet and a stance often bent at the knees when she spoke of something that excited her, as if she were ready to catch a football from some Metal-Wearer hidden in the bushes. She was likeable because she was soft, and a goodness leapt from her mannerisms, shining through her silver-skinned, rubbery features, and it reached those spellbound people around her.

Well, kids, we've got some tough stuff, she said, her voice echoing, as if they were being given a pregame pep talk against a dangerous team. *You know, in my time, the Wizard wasn't always available for consult, even if it was important. You kids are lucky. In my day, we only had the legends to go on. Now, I say we go and see the man. I can get you there a little faster. Stopping time is a serious matter—an offense against the Ruler Unseen, and then there's the matter of the missing hearts.*

*But how did you…*asked Nadia.

Know? she answered. *Well, we're privy to a lot more that goes on than you. Crystal balls and such. Can't control everything, though, so here's the present mess. We'd better get going now,* said the Witch.

The Silver Witch unfolded the quilt, which was now three times the size as the one she had arrived on. They all got up onto the quilt one at a time, hesitant to put weight upon it, but the quilt sprung back and held their weight, as if it had an invisible bed underneath it. Lastly, the Silver Witch jumped onto the corner.

Hold on, she advised. And it was a good thing they did, because when she lifted her nose high in the air and directed upward with a wand, the quilt shot up into the sky.

Once they had reached a height, they leveled out and flew at a steady pace.

What I can tell you is this, she continued. *We do have an advantage, if you can restore them.*

How are we going to do that? asked Nadia.

The Silver Witch looked directly at Nadia. *The Wizard will tell you how you are going to accomplish it.*

Why do you keep saying you? Nadia countered.

You, Nadia. Don't be so surprised, she continued. *Don't you think it's a little strange that you can see through the illusions of the Voice? That's a special power, you know. Special power indeed. It comes from the Ruler Unseen.*

But why do I have it? asked Nadia.

Listen, my dear, she said, pointing her finger in the air, *the fact is you've been regaining your memory gradually. That can only be the power of the Ruler Unseen working through your heart. Nothing else could penetrate so powerful a spell. You see?* she smiled. *It was meant to be this way.*

I don't understand, said Nadia.

Didn't you tell her? the Silver Witch asked Georgeonus.

Georgeonus looked over. His eyes flickered as he shook his head.

The Silver Witch sighed a deep sigh and let her cheeks puff out, as if in preparation to present a challenging scenario.

Nadia, your memory was erased by a spell from Talmus years ago. And your heart was removed. Now if a heart is not restored within three days of its removal, it can't be fully returned. But what happens to it? Well, it takes on permanently the character of the possessor. Which means those children's hearts are going to be black and horrible. They will work all kinds of evil in this world. And the possessor has gained something valuable indeed, by taking that heart. But I don't think your version of things has ever happened before.

What do you mean? Who has my heart? demanded Nadia.

Again the Silver Witch glanced at Georgeonus reproachfully and puffed her cheeks out in a big sigh.

Well, you asked Georgeonus here to remove it, she said, as if it were common knowledge. *And it was a good thing you did, 'cause you'd be a goner by now. Nadia, your heart was left with the Ruler Unseen. Don't you see? It is why you haven't feared Talmus. Because His power resides in you.*

Nadia tried to digest what was being said. At the same time, her insides knew it was the truth. The Silver Witch continued.

Now, how did Georgeonus know how to do that? Where to leave your heart? Truth is, he's a special kind of prince, and he was lucky enough to hang around the Wizard when he was young. The Wizard took him along while visiting his brother, and Professor Krinkle showed Georgeonus the secret places in the underground. Georgeonus knew it was a special place. A sacred place. And I don't think it's an accident that you two ended up there. Something on the line of fate, if you get my drift. These other children, well, said the Silver Witch, staring off gravely, *their hearts are in a very frightening place.* Slowly, an expression of hope grew back into her features. *But what Talmus did not plan, Nadia, is that your heart would be linked to the Ruler Unseen.*

I don't mean to sound ungrateful, but how is that going to help us? asked Nadia.

I'll leave that for the Wizard to tell, answered the Witch.

As they flew with the Silver Witch to see the Wizard, Nadia was a little nervous about visiting him. He seemed to be a powerful, though good, magician. It was he who had given Holofernes crucial information about combating Talmus the Voice with the Lightning spell.

What do we call you? asked Nadia.

You can call me Mabel, said the Witch with a twinkle.

Nadia, so relieved to be receiving information, tried to hide any signs of desperation in her voice and asked, *Mabel, Do I not have any parents, then?*

You were brought down here by the Wizard, she answered. *Have to ask him about that, too.*

As Nadia pondered this in her mind, Georgeonus suddenly remembered the day Nadia had arrived at the castle in the basket. A small child then, he had peered from behind the queen's ornate gown and noticed a silvery substance on Nadia's forehead, which turned to dust and blew away in the wind.

Yep. That was me, said the Silver Witch, watching Georgeonus, who returned her stare. *Couldn't resist a kiss for good luck.*

Will the children be okay once their hearts are restored? asked Nadia.

Well, thought Mabel, *they may be a little off from where they were before.*

How do you mean? asked Nadia.

The Witch winced. *They may become susceptible.*

To what? asked Nadia.

Evil has touched them, touched their very core, she said. *Their hearts will be susceptible to that evil, which has held them in their hands. They'll have a hard time trusting people, because they'll feel they're going to lose their heart again, and I mean in the literal sense. They'll be susceptible to the touch of evil, because it has been in that place. But all things have the ability to heal. So there's still hope.*

The Silver Witch winked, and Nadia felt a wave of reassurance from her powerful and good presence. She didn't want to leave Mabel's side.

CHAPTER V
WIZARD OF HILL COUNTRY

They began to ascend again. Up and up they flew, over the caramel-colored floor toward the distant horizon in the Land of Silence, past the white wall to the western outskirts. The grass and landscape below them became a blur of green and purple as they headed up into the bright air and through fluffy clouds.

The clouds were like a cotton landscape below them, and all traces of land below were gone. Above them, in the distance, was a set of dense clouds tinged with pink resting in the air, and then Nadia gasped, for nestled atop them was a glorious, ancient looking castle of light-grey stone.

They stopped before a grand staircase leading up to a foyer, and standing there at attention was an elderly footman, about four and a half feet tall and dressed in formal castle attire. He graciously approached the quilt to act as valet, and he was very proper, with his eyes half drawn and his chin in the air. Not wanting to offend him by refusing, the Silver Witch helped Nadia off the quilt, and after Georgeonus and Holofernes exited, she surrendered it to his capable hands.

When they entered the castle, the Wizard was already walking briskly toward them from a long hallway, his yellow silk robe with a purple lining flowing behind him, and by the echoing sound of the door that slammed, as well as his footsteps, they realized that there was sound here.

"Well, hello there," he said. "I've been expecting you. Didn't have any trouble finding the place with Mabel, here, I see."

He approached them, his white beard long and lustrous, his eyes a twinkling blue, and his yellow cap sparkling with purple stars.

"Can't stand the silence," he explained. "Not for me. So while you're in here, there's sound."

Holofernes and Georgeonus nodded and gestured a half bow. Nadia looked up at the old wizard. He was lean, vibrant, very tan, and healthy looking, and the tiny wrinkles around his friendly but wise eyes were etched over taut, smooth skin.

"Hello," said Nadia shyly. He nodded and briskly turned to lead them.

They headed into the Wizard's study and observatory. It was a large, circular room, with a giant telescope pointed outward at the domed ceiling. Many curious metal instruments were about, and there were crystal balls of different sizes and colors, a massive desk with papers, ancient manuscripts, a mortar and pestle, and a sitting area with a pastel couch and plush chairs. The Wizard walked past one of the crystal balls mounted on a pillar, followed closely by the Silver Witch. Nadia, Georgeonus, and Holofernes followed.

Inside the crystal was a haze of black smoke swirling like a billowing storm, and amidst the smoke were small red objects which darted willfully and then appeared to be thrown about.

The Wizard heaved a sigh and headed toward the seating area.

"Well, you know you've done a serious thing, stopping time," said the Wizard, sitting. "And you've felt the repercussions of it. But, these are drastic times, when dark magick can only be countered by powerful magick. So, sit, sit," he said, gesturing to the sitting area. "We have many things to discuss, no?"

They sat down, and the Wizard sat on the edge of a chair as he continued.

"A voice is a dangerous thing. But normally, it has no real knowledge of its power, because it never leaves its island. The voices never left the island until now," he said, shaking his head. "But these are shifting times. Talmus is an evil, an evil that shall serve its purpose in cleansing the lands of what the Ruler Unseen hates. But I'm afraid she has caused much pain in the process."

"You make it sound like Talmus is a medicine of some kind," said Nadia.

"Oh, not a medicine. A disease. The medicine is what the people will learn and apply."

"Talmus has used the power of her own powerful voice, to terrorize and almost break apart anyone who heard the full force of it. She has terrorized them mentally—gotten inside their heads and caused them to do things—or threatened them with madness. She has terrorized them physically, actually stealing their voices and ability to communicate. And something else happened. She has become more powerful by possessing their voices, her powers as a Voice have multiplied, and the people are weaker. They did not have the defense of their own voices; they are forlorn without them, with the very act of having surrendered them. It will be the same with the hearts of the next generation, only worse. Talmus will have more will, more fire for her power and her goals, and in turn, the children will wander soulless, lost, in apathy. If you do not restore these children's hearts, I am afraid the souls of future generations shall be lost. They will give birth to a new generation of soulless people. This is only a testing ground for Talmus as her power grows. She will take this evil to other lands—if she has not already. We can't let this go on."

"What can we do?" asked Georgeonus.

"There is magick to remedy it, but it will take more than magick. The people will have to fight. But right now, it is imperative that we save those hearts. Now," he said, very business-like, "you have three days to retrieve these lost hearts." Then his face grew ashen and serious, and looking at the floor he said, "They are in a most horrible and terrifying place, a place no mortal should ever have to visit, for if he— or she—should venture there, he may certainly not return. But alas, you have been given a gift! A power in your pocket, help from above, from the Ruler Unseen himself! Imagine! A power that you must use to complete this dreadful task. And here she is!"

The Wizard looked straight at Nadia.

"I don't understand!" said Nadia, standing. "Would someone please explain all this to me? What do I have to do with this? What does my heart have to do with getting the children's hearts back?" Nadia felt her voice rising to a shout. "Would someone just tell me what is going on?!"

The Silver Witch glanced over at Holofernes and Georgeonus and nodded, and they in turn looked toward the Wizard. Then the three rose and left the hall, leaving the Wizard and Nadia alone.

The Wizard looked at Nadia and smiled warmly. He sat on the couch, and there was compassion, and a bit of admiration, in his expression. Nadia had no idea why he would admire a simple farm girl like herself. She was looking forward to some answers.

"Come here, my child," said the Wizard, patting the couch beside him.

Nadia sat down on the couch. Like the Witch, The Wizard had a great presence and goodness that was palpable. He held deep wisdom in his eyes, and he looked glorious in his layers of silk robes, which spilled luxuriously onto the couch. Nadia looked down, embarrassed at being a simpleton in his presence, and the Wizard touched her chin so that she lifted her head.

"You, my child, are a special one. You were chosen by the Ruler Unseen to come here."

Next to the couch was a pedestal with a large crystal ball with cream-colored smoke swirling slowly within it. He turned and waved a hand at it, and it lifted up into the air and floated toward them. It stopped between them, and Nadia watched it intently.

"Some time ago, a darkness made itself known in my crystal gazing," he said.

The smoke turned pink, and then dark purple, and then black.

"It was slow to take shape, but I saw that it was moving toward the Land of Silence." The smoke concentrated itself in an upper corner of the crystal ball, and a miniature model of the Land of Silence and its castle came into view below it.

"Even if it weren't evil, I knew that we had never had darkness, or storm clouds, in the Land of Silence, so I knew something was amiss."

The black smoke encompassed the dusty road, the white wall, and the castle.

"The people in the Land of Silence are dear to me. I watch over them from my place in the sky here, so it was my job to find out what that was. And so, I went above. Far, far above," he said, gazing upward and then at Nadia, as if telling her a grand bedtime story. "I went to another castle—one so high above, and so large, and with so many rooms that you could never count them all. Do you know where that is?" he said playfully.

Nadia shook her head.

The images that the Wizard described continued to form in the crystal ball, and Nadia watched them, entranced.

"I arrived and got settled from my journey. Then I refreshed myself and dined in the great hall that night. I spoke with the Ruler Unseen's servants, telling them of my concern."

In the crystal, there was a massive fireplace with two high-backed chairs positioned by a great, long dining table. The table was set for one, and the Wizard dined at it. Then, he reclined by the fire. Nadia's expression stilled as she stared at the scene with vague recognition.

"Soon after, I spoke with the Ruler Unseen, or rather, I voiced my concerns to a distant shadow of His reflection, because He is too magnificent and holy to face. Then I retired for the night. The next night, while I was dining by the fire, there was some commotion in the entrance hall. I heard the screaming and weeping of a man and saw the scuffling of many people.

"I couldn't see everything that was happening, but one of the servants told me that they had had a new arrival. I didn't know much about the goings on of the castle, so I didn't ask. But when I looked out, there was a young girl standing by with the servants and watching the whole affair. After the noise died down, one of the servants came in with the little girl, and told me that I would receive help, and could depart the next morning."

Nadia stared at the scene in the crystal, watching the young girl who stared at the Wizard in the hall.

"The next day I was given instructions, and you—a little baby in a basket—were to be taken to the Land of Silence. Mabel delivered you there. The Ruler Unseen said that it was now your destiny to serve Georgeonus, and the King and Queen, and the Land of Silence, and to liberate the people. You have something very special to offer. Something very special indeed. "

The Wizard paused, staring at the little girl in the crystal globe.

"That is you, Nadia," said the Wizard, pointing to the girl. "Do you remember?"

In the globe was a young girl of about seven. It was not Nadia, or at least, it did not look anything like her. The girl had light-brown hair and wore rags that had been cleaned and tended.

"That's not…me," said Nadia unsurely, but when she said it, it felt like an untruth. She didn't remember, but there was something familiar about the girl. She looked up at the Wizard, doubtful. "Is it?"

"Yes. But not in the form you are in now" was his careful answer.

"What do you mean?"

"There is a veil over your memory for that part of your existence. It has to do with your destiny, and where you were before it was all decided."

"But don't I have a right to know what my destiny is? To remember?" she asked.

"Not really," he said, looking up, considering, and then back to her. "If you remembered everything, it might interfere with your mission and with your ability to carry it out. You were selected, but you were also willing." The Wizard pointed with his finger, as if this were an important point.

The Wizard waited for Nadia to take in what he had said and then continued. As he spoke, the scenes within the globe formed.

"Back then, there was a City Survey program that the Ruler Unseen was conducting in certain Lands."

Puffs of white clouded the picture, and then the girl was sitting in an alley, horribly skinny in filthy rags, picking through garbage and feeding an emaciated kitten who clung to her.

"Lands that are connected to the Air Doors that we know of, and some that only the Ruler Unseen is aware of.

You were taken out of one of these lands and brought to His castle, in this upper dimension, as part of the City Survey program."

The scene changed to show the back of a man in a linen robe walking. He carried a waif of a girl, who was passed out in his arms, legs dangling, away from the town and toward the castle. Nadia's eyes took on a distant look, as if she were trying to remember something deep within her soul. Again came puffs of smoke, and the scene changed to the interior hall of the castle. It was nighttime, and the girl was sneaking down a vast staircase toward a blazing fireplace and a table set for one with food.

Nadia stared at the globe with a troubled expression and then down at her hands in her lap. She had hoped that the story of her past would bring answers, but it only held more questions than she could even process at the moment. She suddenly felt as though she belonged to no one. Even though she was supposedly sent to help others, the actual truth was that she did not even have a family of her own. Even if she had her memory back, from this life or the life before, there would be no one there. She was completely and utterly alone.

"But who then is my mother? Where are my parents? Where is my family?" she asked desperately. "I had to come from somewhere!"

The Wizard's face fell. "I can show you, Nadia, who they are, from that life. But you can't expect anything from them. You can't expect to know where they are or anything about their land or the life they lead."

"Why not?"

"Because you have a new life now. It is not wise to look back."

Nadia's eyes filled with tears at this thought. Things weren't getting better about herself. They were getting worse, and more desolate all the time. She was simply looking into the nothingness of her own origin, and it was not amnesia anymore. It was the bitter and painful truth.

The Wizard watched her sympathetically and waved his hand over the crystal globe. The smoke cleared to reveal a large disorganized family living in poor conditions. Numerous children ran about. The mother looked exhausted, and the father yelled at the children. They all wore what looked like their Sunday best; even these were tattered and sun-worn clothes.

"You didn't spend much time with them," said the Wizard. "They wouldn't remember you—at least, not in the form you are in now. If you had stayed with them, it is doubtful that they would have noticed much of you anyway, unfortunately," he said, waving the scene away. "Besides, you never would have fulfilled your destiny."

"These are my relatives, my family?" asked Nadia, standing in disbelief, dismayed by the images now engulfed by cream-colored swirling clouds. Nadia looked at him. "I thought there would be something…Something that I came from, and something I would want to return to. *Something!*"

The Wizard was surprised, and then in a compassionate tone, he said, "You are upset because you have been trying to find out who you are, to regain your memory. But you must remember: we are all alone in this life, truly, from when we are born until our dying breath. Where we came from, our true home, is with the Ruler Unseen—*that* is where are all one family. And we shall all return to Him. What you perceive as your family is your longing for connection. You shall have human connection in this life, and it will surpass anything that they would have given you. I can show you more of your life there, sometime, if you like. Before you assumed this form. Come back and see me. You will come to understand. But right now, you all have a dangerous task ahead, and not unlimited time. I have taken this time with you Nadia because it is necessary for you in your task ahead."

Nadia knew inside that what the Wizard spoke was true, and she tried to forget her own concerns and think about the task at hand. He was right. They had to save the children's hearts. Nadia had been chosen for this. Somewhere inside of her she knew this, and she was comforted to think that she could return to see the Wizard to find out more about her past.

"Yes," she said, wiping her eyes, "I'd like that very much, to come back. Thank you. Thank you for telling me. It's important that I know."

"Why you feel it is desperately important to know about yourself, perhaps more than normal, is because you haven't had your heart. You have been trying to regain your memory, despite the Voice's powerful spell on you. It is because of this destiny of your heart that you were able to see through the Voice's illusions, to know that you had memories that were missing, to be able to fight to regain them and break through the spell. That is no ordinary power. This was the power of your connection to the Heart of the Ruler Unseen. You see, we cannot think our way out of this world of illusions, because our minds are of this world. But with that other tool, which is a gateway to where we come from—the Great Heart, we are able to see much, much more. We are all connected to this great Heart, some more than others, especially if we choose to be. What must happen now, Nadia, is that we get your heart back. Your heart has been in a very special place—it's been in the care of the Ruler Unseen. That means that when you get your heart back, it's not going to be the same."

"It's not?" she asked, tremulously.

"No. Like the children's hearts have been touched by evil, your heart has been touched by the Great Ruler. You will be, in effect, receiving that Heart. It's not going to be easy. It might be painful. You must be careful not to reject it—it could prove fatal. It's like you've gotten a transplant, and there will be a transition period so you'll have to adjust to this foreign organ. New blood, new sensations; it'll be different. But it is precisely what is needed right now. It's going to enable you to rescue the others."

"Where have the hearts gone?" she asked.

"To a horrible place. They've gone into the underworld, and they're being hunted—right now. You'll have to face some challenging things to be able to catch them, and not be caught yourself. It is…the Nithera, the underworld. I'm afraid it's a bottomless place where you could be lost forever."

"It must end somewhere," Nadia reasoned.

"It is bottomless, and its paths and lakes lead you always further downward. There are very dangerous creatures there."

"And if I'm caught?"

"I'm afraid all is lost for them, and you can't come back here. It is a place of great suffering—a cursed place."

"It sounds like I'm going to suffer anyway, getting this Heart back."

"Yes. But in that other place, your soul could be lost, consumed and tortured by horrible things. It's not the same thing. It is hard to find hope there." The Wizard looked into the distance with a weighty expression, and then awe. "Now, with this returned heart, you will see and feel things only the Ruler Unseen sees and feels. You will see and feel great power, and great hope that is needed, but great sorrow, too." The Wizard looked up sheepishly, as if he feared for Nadia. "He has determined that *you* can handle that, Nadia. So you see, it is your destiny," said the Wizard. "For whatever reason, this is what you have been created for. It is what you have come to fulfill. But don't get caught up in it, either. We all like to think that we're special. But the truth is, we're only as special as He makes us. He chose you Nadia, because He had His reasons. Maybe because of something He saw in you, maybe not. I mean, if there was something special there, He created it anyway. So remember that, too. Okay?"

Nadia nodded. She took a breath and stood. "So what must we do?"

The Wizard smiled at Nadia's resolve.

"First, I'm going to renovate that suit," said the Wizard as he inspected the assorted parts of Nadia's copper suit. "Good gracious! This is all scrap."

"What are you going to do?" she asked.

"I'm going to give you a boost, that's all."

Nadia was led to a bright, round chamber constructed out of a white, hard plastic and clear glass. She entered the chamber as the Wizard nodded. He stepped up to a control panel and began to operate buttons. The glass door closed.

Lights brightened and instruments whirred, and when Nadia emerged, she could float on her boots like Georgeonus. Not only was the suit polished, but she could also sense that the suit had been fortified with other powers that might come in handy.

As if on cue, The Silver Witch, Georgeonus, and Holofernes came back into the room.

Holofernes and Georgeonus also charged up their suits, while the Wizard rummaged in a back room. He returned, carrying bow and quivers, handing them to Nadia, Georgeonus, and Holofernes. Holofernes felt the object.

"I can sense much—enough to get around, to fight, to ride—but cannot shoot arrows," said Holofernes, looking troubled.

The Wizard put his hand on Holofernes' shoulder and guided him toward a cabinet. "I think I have something for you in here, my friend. Let's see, now," he said, as he rummaged through a drawer, pushing small objects around.

"Ah!" he said, lifting out a silver box. "Here we are!" the Wizard said, opening it to reveal a blue velvet lining cradling two blue sapphires. "These aren't permanent," he said, handing Holofernes the stones. "But they'll do for now."

In one hand feeling forward, and the other hand trembling to hold the box, Holofernes took the stones. He was so stunned at receiving seeing stones that he merely stood, unsure of what to do.

"Here," said the Wizard, taking them back, and with a wave of his hand before Holofernes' eye sockets, the blue sapphires were inserted, and Holofernes could see. He looked at his hands and then around the room in awe.

"Mind you, I need those back. Don't know if we can find a permanent solution for you. That's a dark curse you've got there. Come back and see me," he said, his arm on Holofernes' shoulder, as a tear rolled down Holofernes' cheek. "We'll figure something out." Georgeonus smiled.

"Now. The only way you're going to make it through the underground is going to be on a wildabeast—a demon dog of the deep. It's the *only* way you can get around in the canyon. Your suit is fast, but it won't be fast enough. There are horrible things down there, and they'll be hunting you as soon as you get there, just as you're hunting those hearts. But first, you'll have to catch one. And then, you've got to get on it. Make no mistake: if you don't get on its back, they will tear you to shreds. Just want you to be prepared."

"How are we doing to do that?" asked Nadia.

"With these," said the Wizard. He removed three bundles of golden arrows from a tall thin wardrobe, along with some rope. "These arrows won't kill them, they'll only make them drowsy—long enough for you to get on."

The Wizard gave Nadia a tiny gilded cage with a door and a handle at the top. "You will put them in here and bring them to me," he said.

They looked doubtfully at the Wizard.

"Don't worry. They'll fit. I've shrunk it. This will protect them." The Wizard clipped the cage to a belt in Nadia's suit.

Georgeonus, Nadia, and Holofernes all nodded.

"And now, my dear," said the Wizard, "we must return that heart of yours."

62

CHAPTER VI
THE WOODEN CHAMBER

A sense of inevitable foreboding now filled Nadia. It was kind of like being called upon by the teacher in school, only hundreds of times worse. Did she even want her heart returned? She had not planned for this detour of getting her heart back, yet it seemed essential to their mission.

"Mabel's going to give you a little salve to help to prepare you for its return," said the Wizard, nodding at the Silver Witch. The Silver Witch looked at Nadia with a mix of pity and admiration.

The Silver Witch walked up to Nadia and motioned her silver finger toward Nadia's chest. Nadia could not tell if the Witch had even touched her physically, but she felt something warm in her heart area, and she realized it was the Silver Witch's magick. There was some silver goo on Nadia's suit. The Witch smiled at Nadia gently but solemnly, and then she lowered her hand.

The Wizard walked them through the hallways toward the front of the castle where the valet could be seen pulling up on the Witch's quilt like a motorcar.

"Thank you, Jules," said the Wizard. "Remember, when you go into the canyon, deeper down, you will know that you are approaching the Sacred Center when the air becomes light, the sand soft. Remove your boots, for this is a holy ground. Tread lightly," he warned, as they climbed onto the quilt, "for you do not know if the Ruler Unseen shall make His thoughts known to you there. Banish all of your own so that you may hear Him."

"Here is the spell reversal," he said, handing Georgeonus a piece of ancient paper sealed with wax. "Just in case you forgot." He sighed and looked at all of them as they prepared to ride away.

"You've got two days."

In no time they were back in the canyon of Standhøfl Tourdemil. They descended low into the depths and landed on the flat earth amidst amber rocks. Nadia recognized it as that sacred place where years before, she and Georgeonus had removed their boots to step onto soft, ultrafine sand, to approach and tread upon what they knew to be holy ground. It was the outskirts of a place of peaceful quiet that existed unlike any she had known, the place where she had lapsed into forgetfulness, and where her heart had been taken away.

Once they had dismounted from the quilt, Nadia was unsure of which way they were headed. All was quiet around them, and they were very near the soft sand. Georgeonus unfurled the scroll. But the Silver Witch looked at Nadia with a pitying expression as she removed from her black folds a wand of bent wood with a precious clear stone at its tip.

"What is it?"

"Will you let me, Nadia, save you from some of this pain?"

"Okay, Mabel. If you think it will be painful."

"It will be. But you will remember most everything else. We cannot go with you, but we'll be here when you return," she said.

"Very well," said Nadia, and she had butterflies of excitement, thinking of having her heart back.

The Witch approached Nadia and raised the wand to rest on Nadia's forehead, above the space between her eyes.

The air grew dark; the world around Nadia began to twist and fall away; and the last thing Nadia saw was the Silver Witch, Georgeonus, and Holofernes disappearing through a dark hole.

She was still standing, but everything was dark, and the surroundings were tinged red. There was a dull hum coming from somewhere, but she did not know where. It was virtually undetectable, but pleasant, like angels sustaining a note. She remained, waiting. Nothing. All was dark. She lifted her hand before her face, trying to see it in front of her.

"Hello?" Nadia asked, tentatively stepping. As she spoke, she thought she heard an echo, like a door closing. She waited. Again the sound came, louder this time, and she ran toward it into the dark, senses heightened, reaching her arms, fearing what she may run into. She groped, sometimes running and then stopping in fear. Louder and louder the wooden door slammed, like a distant, sporadic, foreboding drum, intermittent in its pace. This could not be the canyon. Where was she?

Far ahead, she could see the glow of a tunnel entrance hardly lit. She shuffled toward it, and she discerned that its dim interior was a corridor of wood.

Oak. There was no indication of what this corridor attached to in the darkness. The outside walls were swallowed up by the mouth of the darkness, not ending, not beginning anywhere, not giving her a clue as to this tunnel's purpose, except for the door at its far end. The crack under its frame revealed an orange light source. The walls were rounded and revealed no edges, no endings; they only swooped upward as she ran her fearful fingers along the strange, swelling, smooth shape which disappeared from sight.

Stepping in, she saw that the corridor narrowed toward the door ahead. There, the well-worn, splintered oak door stood tightly jammed, its dry, pale facade uninviting. Its handle was plain: round, brass, a silver metal under element at its worn contours. Nadia tentatively stepped, checking behind, half expecting the corridor to move, warp, or swallow her whole and cease her existence. The door too seemed alive as an intimidating, palpable energy that travelled down the hallway, scrutinizing her movement forward. Was this a duel, a confrontation, and aberrant that the door—this dry, compacted splinter—should have personality? She half expected it to move, to fall forward in opposing attack, to swell in its middle and explode into jagged, shooting toothpicks, impaling her in the front at a thousand points. Approaching, she thought she perceived the midsection of the door breathing, as if tempted by her thought. Now closer, she reached her hand toward the handle, like a peace offering, for she felt the door was shocked at her approach and prepared to react. Though her hands were shaking, her legs urged her onward.

Suddenly the door flew open, and a force of air threw her back, sending her sliding back along the wooden floor. Once again submerged in the darkness, she heard a palpitating, quickened rhythm: what sounded like the steady beating of an immense heart.

Slam! The door closed with a deafening echo, and the air suctioned back, like a valve pulling oxygen through after spitting out toxic refuse. The oak door opened again softly, and as Nadia rose, it slammed, opening and closing in furious, quick, threatening bursts, as if in fight mode.

Nadia was not sure how she could make it into the next room, or why, but something invited her, despite the door's threatening darts. She knew that the underlying, generating fuel for such quickened action was fear, and she took it as a bluff as she charged the door. The door seemed affronted as she grasped the corridor and advanced toward its handle, ignoring the spasmodic opening and closing.

Slam! Slam! Slam! Slam! Slam!

Grabbing hold of its handle, her whole body was jerked upward at first and then in spastic movements, into an abrupt slam! against the frame, pushed and pulled. Never was Nadia so aware of the sinews that held her arm to her shoulder bone. She gripped the handle with two hands and then slipped her leg into the frame, crying out in pain as she was slammed in the door's closing. She braced the door jamb with one hand as the door beat her in its presence.

A final slam on Nadia's wrist sent her doubled over, bracing her hand between her thighs, cursing the door, and in the next moment Nadia was in the next room.

A room that was not a room but another, slightly smaller, corridor.

Looking up, she could see that the hallway was filled with an orange glow, and the door at its end was a sienna-toned chestnut wood, less worn, less splintered but still broken in. As she approached this new door, it whooshed open and then slam! It closed, fueled by a lapping current of air on its other side. It was less threatening, more rhythmic and sweeping than the oak door, which continued its raucous in intermittent fury.

Compared to the oak door, this door was gentle, and Nadia stepped into the orange light and proceeded forward. As she grabbed its handle, it pulled and pushed her, sending her legs in a pleasant upswing of air as she grabbed hold, eventually wedging her leg toward its frame, suffering gentler aerated blows.

On this went, and Nadia travelled, bungling and bruised, through three more corridors, each less threatening. The rooms became deeper, reddened hues, the corridors closer, the doors smaller, richer in color, the wood darker, less dry. Indeed, as she progressed into the fifth, the wood of the corridor and doors exuded moisture and felt wet, as if filled with blood. She felt light headed, and all the while, a rhythmic heart beat that she had heard in the darkness grew louder. She imagined that this red-soaked room was the last chamber, listening to the relentless pound, pound, pound, pound, pad along—loud, near, as if its source were on the other side of the mahogany door ahead, whose soft, valve-like openings and closings sent forth a warm, dizzying, oxygen-rich air. Nadia looked into the dark of the room behind it, wondering what her going further would mean. She wondered of her return from this claustrophobic, chambered house, if she were to be caught in its vessels, lost or suffocated in a linear arterial maze should the doors cease their activity.

The red door did not slam, but only flapped through a well-worn jamb slightly, swinging to its other side before returning and opening. Its movement over the soft, meshed floor mimicked exactly the heartbeat sound, and Nadia pushed it open, anticipating its regularity, but sending a skipped beat into the rhythm.

As she entered, the palpitations quickened.

There stood Georgeonus, holding in his white hands her heart, just as he had stood in the canyon that day. He exuded a smile in the glow of his face, his features not moving, his eyes a dimmed, respectful glow. He carefully moved closer, offering the beating organ on his bloodied, white skin, gingerly cupping it as it palpitated louder, and then he disappeared. She was alone in the room, but Nadia felt an immense Presence watching, like that day in the canyon when she asked that her heart be removed. It was overwhelming, and she felt that she should prostrate herself on the floor of the closet-like room, but could hardly move.

Then there was a Voice that spoke to her within, without words. She saw that these corridors did exist, somewhere inside her. Indeed, they were all the doors that she had constructed, closed and slammed to keep out the Ruler

Unseen. Somehow she had known Him all along—before the Land of Silence, and she swelled with anger. Nadia felt her eyes fill up with hot tears. She could not remember ever feeling so alone, and at the same time so watched, so afraid, and yet so comforted. In an instant she came to understand the reason for her existence in the Land of Silence, why she had been sent, the reason her heart and memory had been removed, the reason for its return—the reason for everything. She realized that she was still the orphan who had lived on the streets, the girl selected and taken into the castle high in the sky, the girl who had been remade into Nadia and sent to the Land of Silence, the one who had slept on the stone floors, the one who could see through the illusions of the Voice, the one banished to the farm and then brought back. She'd been sent to be a part of these people, their history, and their fate.

But she saw that she was also more.

She saw that there was nothing wrong with her being an orphan. It too, had its purpose in helping her to become who she was. The Ruler Unseen had fashioned her for this, and now she must fulfill it. She no longer cared if it made her either chosen, special, ordinary, or cursed. She was who she was as the Ruler Unseen had made her, and her part in it was to take His Hand, to accept her role in this mysterious dance, and to walk the steps lain before her. She stood listening to the quickened heart, feeling faint from all the oxygen, torn between wanting to prostrate herself on the floor in respect, but not wanting to move because she could feel the most inexplicable Power all around her, watching her, infusing her with—what she knew to be the most powerful force in all of the universes: the power of love. And she had been given this gift—the gift of this moment. It was with her, gazing at her in this moment.

Georgeonus came back into view. He was still standing there with the heart. Then in an instant the heartbeat faded, and darkness surrounded her—and in it she gasped. All became dark and cold, she felt as if her ribcage had been ripped open, and her voice squelched in a backdraft of air. There was a sharp pain in her chest and a hearty pounding, and she heard herself continuing to gasp for air. Then it felt as if the flesh and bones of her chest was knitting itself back together, and she was soon aware that she was lying on her back. She could not move, but suddenly she could breathe freely, and patches of light swirled around her dizzying head.

And there inside of her was the beating sound. Pumping like a busy, diligent clerk resuming business, as if it had never gone. There was light, pain, and behold: her busy little heart. Only it did not feel so little. It felt different: stronger, larger. A dull, new ache sat in her chest as she lifted her arms for relief, searching for more air. Her hands were caught by other hands and above, coming into view, was a circle of heads looking down upon her in the canyon: Georgeonus, in silver metal with glowing eyes, Holofernes, in gold, with his new sapphire stone eyes, and the Silver Witch, her gooey, metallic skin reflecting in the ethereal glow of the mineral-rich canyon.

As she was helped to stand, unsteadying pains shot through Nadia's chest as this new, great Heart adjusted to her body. Her feet met the ground, and even though she breathed normally, she gasped at sharp bits of cold air that knifed her lungs. But she could do nothing save breathe, holding firmly to the offered arms while standing on the dirt road. She was glad to feel the steady hands in her own, the strong supports at her elbows. The Silver Witch lifted her finger toward Nadia's chest, and she could feel again the Witch's cooling silver salve on the hot pain. It lessened the pain, but it was also like the comfort of a friend, and Nadia understood now how the magick was meant to ease her suffering. The residual goo on her suit turned to sparkling, silver dust trailing into the air.

For the first time in a long time, Nadia felt like herself. All of her memories returned. She was surrounded by those familiar faces that she knew well and now remembered. She could feel the deeper, long-standing affection she had for her companions. Gone was the woodenness of her amnesia and the apathy she had about the people of these lands, and returning were quiet pangs of emotion, which she was familiar with, and which tugged at her heart. In the back of Nadia's mind, pacing like a restless hound, was still the deeper curiosity to one day uncover her other life that had been obliterated. But that life had not been taken wrongly from her. She trusted the Ruler Unseen, not the Voice.

There was something else, too. It touched her like waves that were growing and building with her own memories. It was that Power that Nadia had felt in the blood-filled chamber. Like a storm gathering out of nowhere, Nadia began to experience waves of perception in her heart. In that moment, as she stood there hand in hand with her friends, Nadia glimpsed eternity inside the Ruler Unseen's Heart. It was like a millions hearts and all of their sorrows, all of their joys, and memories had been opened up to her. All of the grief over all of the crimes done against the most innocent of beings—no matter how small—was there laid before her. Yet she knew that it was not the Silver Witch's doing. It was the company that her heart kept, with the Ruler Unseen. When she contemplated this Presence in her newly restored heart, it ached within her, too tender to bear. But there was no escape or turning from it! So Nadia looked into it.

In that instant, inside the Ruler Unseen's Heart, Nadia glimpsed eternity. In that instant, she ventured through all space and time, to the furthest universes, and saw that all was encompassed there, in this Great Heart.

She saw too, that every wound of every being on the earth existed within the Heart, and in this Heart, these wounds had left a mark in its perfect flesh. All the hurts and harms, from every unkind word to every atrocity, all the violent abuses and bloody crimes, from the smallest of lies to the cruelest of tortures, all these things Nadia glimpsed in an instant. No matter whose pains they had been, upon what creature, or in how hidden a manner they had been inflicted, the Ruler Unseen not only knew these offenses but had an identical wound in His own Heart.

But there was the Power, too! That vast power residing within her now that Nadia hardly knew what to do with. She did not merely feel great compassion for humanity but a power she did not fully understand, and like the metal suit, she hardly knew how to begin to direct such a force. Her heart overflowed with a love that seemed to burn and threaten to consume her—to obliterate her by the force of some mysterious fire.

One moment, she felt a great weight in her chest, as if she could understand all of the sorrow of the world. And not just understand it. She was experiencing it right along with whoever was suffering. The next moment, or at the same time, she was not laden down with this burden, but her heart was overflowing with a power she could scarcely grasp.

And just when she thought the feelings had stopped, another wave of sorrow filled the space of her heart, and then filling her whole body, it was sending sorrow up her throat as her eyes brimmed with tears. Nadia dropped to her knees on the canyon floor.

"I cannot—I cannot bear all of that pain!" she cried. "It is too much…too much to bear," she said, reaching for the ground, as the tears fell from her eyes and landed underneath her.

"You can, Nadia," the Silver Witch responded, grabbing her arm and shaking her. "That is why you were chosen. Give it a few moments. Besides," said the Witch, I have given you a powerful magickal salve to prepare you for receiving this very magnificent gift."

"I cannot imagine that you have lessened the pain!" cried Nadia. "I…cannot do this. Not yet."

The Silver Witch put her hand on her hip, as if remembering that she had been insulted. "And why would you want to give back the richness that the Ruler Unseen has to share with you? Hmm? And there is something else there—I know you see it. You must focus on it now."

Nadia thought about this, and then she focused again on the Power that was also lurking there, which she did not yet understand. But the sadness returned.

"Yep. It's tough stuff, kiddo. But you've been given a great gift: a privilege to glimpse the sorrows of the Ruler Unseen. Just imagine how *He* feels!"

Nadia stood.

"Now you have a task to do, remember?"

As she focused on the Power, the pain in her heart subsided, and she felt her strength quickly return; and no sooner did she know it, she was instantly standing tall, and her armor was glowing, and she had a fierce look in her eyes.

In fact, they all jumped back a bit, and the Silver Witch laughed, saying, "That's the spirit!"

Nadia snapped the quiver onto her armor and hoisted the rope around her shoulder.

"Which way to the underground?"

CHAPTER VII
THE NETHER REGIONS

They returned to Utsiket Sorghäven and arrived on a special island which would lead them into the underground. Along the way, they munched on some wafer cookies that Mabel had given them to eat. She said it was *magick sleep*, and rather than giving them energy in their sleep-deprived state, the magick gave them, instead, a kind of packaged sleep so that they felt rested and ready for the day ahead. They washed them down with some invigorating Land of Silence water that Holofernes carried in a canteen. About ten minutes after Nadia ate the cookies, she did indeed feel that she had a night's rest.

Once below, they travelled through the underground by flight: Georgeonus in his special suit, Nadia and Holofernes with the gift of flight in theirs given by the Wizard. Holofernes scanned the surroundings below with wonder; he could now see with his newly acquired eyes.

They travelled down, down, and down: past stalactite caves, past what resembled the faces and limbs of tormented figures in the rock face below, past crevices and pockets where they thought the bottom of the canyon was, only to find that what was revealed was yet another hillside, knoll, narrow passageway or a wide-open area with an eventual cliff at its edge leading further down. They travelled down until they reached an area that they sought, where the air took on a reddish hue, and there were lakes of black water.

The lake that they sought was unavoidable. It was contained in an area that deceived them, that looked indeed as if they had reached the bottom of the canyon. Yet, as the Wizard had told them, it had a hidden access point. The further one walked, the more convinced one was that the area was enclosed. But the Wizard had told them to keep walking toward the end wall. At first nothing happened, and they thought that they would simply come up against the wall. But as they continued on, either a magickal portal opened up, or they were standing in the midst of a great optical illusion: for all the walls shifted, and a faint light revealed a space between the corner of two walls. This was it!

As they walked through it, a deeper canyon was revealed, one that was the point of no return. The Wizard had told them that once they entered this area, they were entering Nithera, the underworld of the dead, where no living beings dwelt, and where their bodies would be fair game to the attacks and hunting of creatures that served the underworld—creatures that tortured the souls who were sentenced here and who could not escape. Because the souls of the condemned sentenced here could not die, they were eternally tortured. And to these creatures, the living flesh of Nadia, Georgeonus, and Holofernes were like tantalizing treats newly lain out at a buffet.

There was the smell of sulfur in the air. It smelled like a mine, where the fumes of metals had been released through toil and the breakage of rock. Nadia smelled something else, and was startled, for at first she did not understand what it was. It was a clean smell like fresh air, and it came occasionally from her own body as they travelled, and she realized that her soul had a scent. Despite her manifold faults, her soul smelled clean, and she was suddenly aware of it. Perhaps it was all the cleaner against this horrible place, and she looked upward as she wondered how far her scent carried to creatures that swam like sharks in this deep.

They had traveled for much of the day, and it was now late afternoon. It was quiet when they came upon a rocky shore and stared into another black-water lake, which stretched ahead. They could not see into the cavernous distance and did not know how to call the ferryman. The Wizard had given them fare: silver pieces which Georgeonus shook rhythmically in the burlap pouch he had been given. As they stood staring at the distance, listening to him jangling the heavy coins, they began to see something emerge. It sailed toward them like an unreal thing, like an apparition, and Nadia thought she could see through both the boat and its rider. It was there, but it wasn't, and the cloaked figure was seated, seemingly driving the vessel forward by sheer will alone. All took on the hues of the canyon: a dark sienna-mud color, which pervaded the boat, the black cloak, and even their metal suits. As the figure approached, it took on a more solid appearance, and then it stood. There was mass under the fabric in the shape of a wiry human figure, but they could see neither face nor hands under the cloak.

The boat landed on the shore, and a bony arm reached toward Georgeonus, who offered the silver into the emaciated hand. It turned and moved toward the other end of the boat, seemingly identical in its helm and prow, and it perched there steadily, gazing ahead. Nadia, Georgeonus, and Holofernes climbed in. They sat behind the figure and peered ahead into the darkness.

The last time Nadia had been on a boat had been the first time she had been on a boat: she was wearing Georgeonus' suit and was seated across from the giant Tars, rowing away from the shore in the open night sky. Now she looked at the back of the specter, its black cape still. What sort of entity was this? What history had its eyes seen? What tasks had it been assigned by an Almighty authority, and were all these not for the higher good? As she contemplated its existence, it turned sharply, and in what was a shadowy hole, where she had glimpsed the fleeting profiles of a skull, she saw the hole suddenly widen into a vast nothingness. As if in answer to her query, this servant appeared to her not as its own being, but merely an aspect of something larger and necessary; its cloak rendered in a familiar shape to appease earthbound beings.

Nadia pulled back her gaze and caught her breath—searching the planks of the boat like plots of earth, as if by digging into them with her eyes she could feel the solidity of life on Earth, or hide from the horror she began to feel as they progressed into a forsaken place. Overhead, she glimpsed lettering carved on the rock as they passed under it: *In Necem Ibis* (You will go to death).

Suddenly their task seemed humanly impossible.

Georgeonus and Holofernes must also have been feeling the unsettling dread that advanced around them, and it became so dark that they lost their bearings on direction: on what was around them, and what they headed toward. There was no natural air here, which could give them clues as to their surroundings, only an acrid smell of mineral, and the overwhelming feeling that they had entered a realm where all of the rules had changed. They were unprotected here—fair game—for they had entered this forbidden place by their free will, and they were now vulnerable to creatures who knew it well.

They approached a graveled shore of a dark-grey, finely ground mineral—like coal mixed with malachite and ground fine. It sparkled in rare places, and they found the light source to be a torch suspended on a rock cliff. As they came onto the shore, the ferryman faded before their eyes, and when they had all exited the boat and turned to watch it move away, he was at its other end.

The only way forward was into a cave, so Georgeonus grabbed the torch from the wall, and they headed in. Even with the torch, it was hard to see what was in front of them, and there were murmurings around them. When Nadia turned her head to listen, it was silent. They stayed close together, trying to remember their task, trying to fight the despair that encroached in on them the further they willingly walked into this poisonous, confined lair.

So they were relieved to see before them yet another canyon. But there was something different about it. Instantly Nadia had the feeling that she was approaching an arena, like those she had learned about in school, where people were tortured, and others would watch as a type of entertainment. She could never understand what type of humanity would find such misery to be sport or entertainment, and she had assumed that it was only a part of primitive humanity's past.

Georgeonus and Holofernes must have sensed danger, for Georgeonus abandoned the torch, and they scouted what might be behind and beside them by stepping back to back and circling, reaching for weapons. Many things happened at once then, and they knew they had to be quick on their feet if they were to capture some demon dogs, before they themselves were captured. First, large shadows hovered over them, and strange forms began to surround them in sweeping motions, ducking and hiding. Then, they could see all sorts of creatures coming at them from distances: in the air, and from all sides.

They were outnumbered.

Holofernes was already on the heels of a demon dog, who turned and bared its fangs in a threatening roar. Nadia and Georgeonus could not help Holofernes, for they too were being targeted. There was no protection for Nadia from either Georgeonus or Holofernes. They were all on their own, and all at once she realized the uselessness of her small frame, but she took refuge in the Great Heart within her.

Georgeonus used his suit to propel himself into the air as a dog ferociously pursued him, growling, jumping, and snapping its jaws. Meanwhile, a flying creature, which looked like a combination of a bat and a tetradactyl screeched and pursued Nadia. The creature was gaining on her, and she quickly rallied and pulled the correct arrow from the quiver, scanning for the nearest dog.

The dog stalking Holofernes would have lunged at him, but Holofernes was quick in the suit. Holofernes catapulted himself over the dog, who then leapt in the air and intercepted him. Holofernes landed on his back amongst the jagged rocks with both arms trying to fend off the dog from lunging at his throat. He was bleeding, but continued to embrace the challenge of the dog. Georgeonus was being closed in on too, no matter how fast he flew. Two dogs and three flying creatures were close, and he was so busy trying to evade their grasp that he could not prepare the arrow.

Holofernes, bleeding and dirty, triumphed over the dog he was fighting with long enough to draw an arrow, but was attacked by five more. Meanwhile, Nadia was not sure which would reach her first: two demon dogs or the flying bat-like creature, its fangs exposed. Nadia saw that they were simply too many, too fast, and without knowing what she was doing, she put her hands over her heart.

A shot of electricity thousands of times more powerful than Georgeonus' suit entered her palms, and instinctively she directed it outward at the creatures. Bolts shot from her, and the creatures around them were stunned and paralyzed. Georgeonus and Holofernes quickly recovered themselves and their quivers. They were surprised, and at first thought the blast had come from somewhere else, until they saw Nadia's glowing palms. The expressions on the creatures' faces showed something like bliss.

Nadia picked up her quiver. Holofernes, dumbfounded, dragged two floating dogs away, and Georgeonus grabbed one. They ran for cover on a crag of rock, which they hoped would give them enough distance them once the effect wore off. Nadia watched them, and she was surprised to feel—and perhaps it was the Great Heart observing—pity for these creatures. They lived in this wasteland underground in what kind of existence for survival? Feeding off fear and any last traces of hope brought from the upper world.

"We must choose a dog now, quickly," she said, knowing that the effects would not last forever.

She was right. Some of the creatures started to move about in their floating state. Nadia aimed her arrow, and Georgeonus and Holofernes followed suit.

The golden arrows found their targets, and each hit the throat area, turning into golden collars once struck. The dogs lay down, and Nadia, Georgeonus, and Holofernes rushed to mount them. Nadia was not at all thrilled to be riding this beast; she would have much preferred a ferocious cat. But she dared not show Georgeonus and Holofernes her trepidation.

Now they had a new set of challenges. First, a giant dog, no matter how giant, is not an easy thing to ride. Second, the other creatures would still be after them. Third, they did not know where they were going. But what they found out, when they finally got the dogs to move, is that a tamed demon dog has instincts and memory like a regular dog, and they led the way to some central place. Surely the hearts would be there. They *had* to be there, because they were running out of time.

Apparently Georgeonus and Holofernes trusted where the dogs were headed, for they took this opportunity to punch and take aim at the creatures that pursued them. They did not approach Nadia, perhaps because they remembered her blast. This went on for a time, until the pursuing creatures were either defeated or could not keep up with the dogs.

When they thought of the cave they had entered and then being outnumbered by the creatures, it paled in comparison to the place they approached. It was a round chasm, dark and cold. It looked like a crater that had been hit long ago with an immense explosion. Now there was an eerie silence here, and everything about it felt wrong.

It was like when something bad happened: when someone got hurt, or an accident occurred. In those situations, one feels the inevitability of the event. Something bad has happened, and it cannot be undone. Adrenaline courses through the veins as one tries to assist the person in dealing with it, or while helping the people around the accident deal with it. It was the same feeling. Things were all wrong here in this crater, and they could not turn back the clock. They were forced to deal with whatever horrible thing was there, here and now, and the adrenaline was coursing through their veins.

Only, there was nothing there.

Or so they thought.

There was a small, dark hole way down at its center. And as the dogs navigated and jumped ever toward it, she thought she could hear the faint screams of children.

Was it in her head? Was she going mad? There was no sound. Just an icy coldness. Georgeonus and Holofernes must have heard it too, for they all looked at each other. Her heart felt heavy, as a great darkness weighed down upon it, like a shadow obliterating any hope and lightness of life. The closer they came, the more they felt a wind blowing around them in a counter-clockwise direction, pulling them down toward the hole.

It was dark. The dogs stopped and cowered, and Nadia, Georgeonus, and Holofernes dismounted. They walked carefully toward the hole. It felt like the edge of the earth, and that if they fell through the hole, they might never be seen nor heard from again.

But when they looked in the hole, they saw a spiral void which continued down. The hearts were there, stuck, clinging, embedded into the edges of the hole like mussels in an ocean cove. There was another opening below, and a bottomless drop beyond that.

The hole was not large enough for Holofernes or even Georgeonus to fit into. The hearts were too far down. If she could reach down, she would, but she knew she would have to remove her metal and be lowered into it in order to retrieve the hearts.

After much discussion, they agreed to lower Nadia into the hole, tethered by a rope.

And so, surrendering her metal beside Georgeonus, down Nadia went feet first into the spiral void.

The further Nadia was lowered in, the more dread she felt. It was as if she were dying, but she knew that she was still breathing.

There were things pulling at Nadia from underneath, and when she realized there was no power in her hands, because her heart was failing, she panicked. The more she panicked, the more anger rose in her at the creatures below, until she could feel no pity for them at all. She focused on the task at hand: the children's hearts. But even this was disheartening, for each heart held the desperate screams for survival. One by one she extracted them, reassuring them in low tones, but it was really herself she was trying to reassure. She placed them into the cage, where they were sucked into once she opened its door, and the hearts were transformed into tiny red, flapping wings, settling on perches as purple-red blobs.

But were not out of the canyon yet.

In the hole, the wind whipped around Nadia as her heart failed. She could not see the end of the drop below, and gazing at it made her feel hopeless that she would ever be brought up again. The creatures darted in at her, snapping and then retreating, trying to make her lose her balance. As long as Holofernes and Georgeonus held the rope, they were her lifeline. They and the Great Heart, though it did not appear to be helping now. Once she had gathered all the hearts, she realized she had to ascend, and she was in such a state of despair that she tugged on the rope. She wondered if the Great Heart had abandoned her, if it could not exist in this place. Did He not exist everywhere? Did He not rule over all? As Georgeonus and Holofernes pulled her up, she tried to fend off the creatures with a blast of her palm, but it short circuited, and nothing emerged.

She reached the top of the opening and passed Georgeonus the cage. Georgeonus reached for it, and for Nadia, as Holofernes pulled up the rope. Suddenly, two creatures were on her: one on her back, chewing on the rope, and one on her side holding her down. By the faintest light coming from above she caught a glimpse of its hideous face, and whatever strength she may have had left failed. It was a horrid face, not just in its features, but in the chilling fact, which registered in Nadia's heart in an instant: that there was no redemption left for this creature. Nadia had glimpsed evil before. She had gazed upon its face, with and without the heart of the Ruler Unseen existing within her, and she knew that even in the face of evil, there was hope. Hope that had once been and hope that could be again were what caused a turn to evil to be healed. But in searching this creature's face, she could not see any hope. She could not see any redemption, and it was difficult to search for it, because it was more horrible than evil. What she had been feeling in these lower canyons—the loss of hope, redemption, the complete loss of the soul, and the pathway that led back to the Ruler Unseen—had somehow been erased from memory entirely, and no pity or mercy from the Ruler Unseen would matter.

The creatures had not only chosen to not return but there was nothing left in them that would make it possible.

That creature, and most here, had not merely succumbed to evil but it had given itself over to it to be consumed; it had forfeited its soul in some type of raw deal and forfeited its only currency to returning to itself as the Ruler Unseen had intended. It was simply a shell now for pure evil.

And this was why no creatures ventured here: because they could be consumed by this venom and not return. What could be done to stop this? Why did this place exist? It was beyond her understanding. What could Nadia do? She had not merely her old, feeble small heart, but the heart of the Ruler Unseen. It must count for something.

In that moment, as Georgeonus lifted the cage and she let it go, something caught hold of her arm, and the rope also fell away from underneath. One had chewed it away, and they both took hold of her. Georgeonus and Holofernes panicked. Georgeonus put the cage down, and they grabbed hold of Nadia's shirt, but they looked into the faces of the creatures and lost all strength, like Nadia, faced with all that the creatures were.

"Go!" said Nadia. "Get the hearts to the Wizard!"

Georgeonus' eyes shone a blinding light, but then flickered, and Holofernes tried to fight the creatures, but his strength waned.

"I'll be all right," said Nadia to Georgeonus, looking into his eyes. "Don't wait for me. I'll be okay. The Ruler Unseen will know what to do. Get Holofernes back. I will find you." And at that, Nadia was pulled away, down and down, the memory of the anguish in their faces, of horror and hopelessness, and the despair of this wretched place seared into her inner vision.

Nadia knew that if her heart had not been joined to the Ruler Unseen's, she would feel that in this moment, she were truly dying. It would not matter that her body was not yet dead, for simply the sight of these creatures brought utter terror to her soul. Gazing into their faces and being handled and carried away by them was certain death; there was a knowing that she could lose her own soul—that the misery and the eternality of this place where no one would venture help might cause her to bargain for anything in order to escape torment.

But in this moment, she was not there. The Great Heart dwelt within her in the space of her own, so now she simply gave herself over to it completely, for there was no hope for her mortal being now, or her mortal heart. How would the Ruler Unseen view these creatures? Were they that far gone? Could their souls ever be brought back?

Down they went. Just when she thought they must surely reach bottom somewhere, somehow, they penetrated another layer of the void. There was no landscape left; it was simply a tunnel leading down. Its edges were remarkably well hewn, like metal, perhaps bartered as work, or made to pass the countless hours of eternal sentences. As they slowed, she noticed a wind and remembered the time in Standhøfl Tourdemil when time stood still: that eerie, directionless idle wind which rebuked in the lashes of its gusts, searched with futile purpose the places it touched, and echoed infinite torment in its long whistles.

Suddenly they touched down. The creatures landed gracefully, and Nadia could see a cavernous floor, lit by a dim orange light. There was no less dread here; she knew that she would be brought before some ruler in this realm. Whenever the shadow of her small heart trembled in agony, fear, and despair for her mortal life, she gave it over completely to the large Heart of the Ruler Unseen, who had now apparently taken charge. It was like horse and rider, moving as one, sensing every flicker of movement and stimulus: every instinct was on alert.

A foot contacting her back and sending her scrambling forward told her which way she should walk, and the creatures followed. It was a cavernous castle, with much dust settled there. The wind sounded distant, for here all else was still. Nadia continued to walk through a rock corridor, and she wasn't sure the creatures were still there. A glimpse proved they were, hanging back as she approached a throne room. The hair on Nadia's neck prickled, and she felt a sense of mortal dread, but she was checked again by the large Heart, where there was none.

There was an entity there. He was large, about ten feet tall, seated amidst intricate carvings, and in the carvings were so many small squares: moving images. There was too much to take in. There was a strange smell: fragrant and repulsive at the same time. The creature wore a beautiful tailored suit. He had curved horns, hooves, and sharp teeth. There was a glow about him that entranced her, but what captivated Nadia were his eyes. They appeared green, but changed color, and contained such a vast intelligence of the ages, of so many things, that Nadia had an urge to prostrate before him, not in worship, but deference. This he expected, but the Heart of the Ruler Unseen caught Nadia, and her prostration became a respectful bow. The creature seemed affronted but accepted this gesture, for he was studying Nadia, knowing there was something different in her—different from the countless others who had been brought here before. Again Nadia gazed into those eyes—the eyes of the ages—and the Ruler Unseen in her gazed back: an ancient recognition. The creature rose.

Nadia was lifted into the air by a vigorous force and then steadied and brought to equal height to the creature's face. He gazed upon the Presence in Nadia, reading her life history, and all that had happened, in moments. Delight spread across his features, like one who delights in a new story, when all the same stories have been told. But the delight was couched in something sinister: his intelligence, his nature, the stench of mounting evil, the ice that had hold of his cold, stone heart.

"No, Nadia. There is no heart in me. Is that what you are wondering?"

Nadia stared at this ancient creature, stunned and captivated in its gaze. She realized that her mortal person could easily be captivated and held with the smallest effort— entranced and controlled. There was a beauty within him, which she did not fully understand. She only knew it was utterly arresting, but what was hidden from her gaze was its distortion. He did not entertain thoughts of her, for she was only a speck, and too small a game. However, with the heart of the Ruler Unseen, her perceptions were heightened, and she was not so easily fooled. To the creature this was of interest too: a larger game, more of a challenge, and higher stakes.

Nadia did not respond. She had given over to the Ruler Unseen. But it was she who was in charge of her speech, not the Ruler Unseen.

"Speak!" he said, and she saw that it was a disrespect not to answer him, especially in this realm.

"Yes."

"Well. You have brought something special to me, have you not?"

Again Nadia hesitated, waiting for the Ruler Unseen, but quickly she chimed in.

"No."

"No? Is that not why you have come? To offer me something?"

"No."

"I think you misunderstand your adventure, then. Your purpose here. The price you did not plan to pay."

Nadia realized in this moment that she had nothing to lose. She could not match this intelligence—or could she? She had a courage that was not her own. But she must think quickly and stand her ground.

"I have not ventured here to wager anything" was her response.

The entity searched her face. The eyes only entertained this speck of life because of the presence of the Ruler Unseen, and her gumption. But it had seen gumption before. It had spent centuries enduring people trembling before him, pleading.

"You surely have. You have entered my realm, trespassed, and stolen my property. Surely you must know there is a cost for this. Come now, Nadia."

"But they do not belong here. They were stolen, and not rightfully yours."

"You misunderstand a great deal, child of Man. They are mine, Nadia. Do not doubt it. Do you think that these are the first ones to be taken? Talmus works with me. If your form did not contain that Magick object, I would set you on fire."

"If I may ask, what are you called, Sir?"

"I am Lux. And now, you must give me that heart of yours, I'm afraid, and leave this world, for I see that it is very special indeed."

"Wait. What will you do with a heart of the Ruler Unseen?" she asked, stalling for time.

He was momentarily caught off guard, as if he could not completely possess or read the Great Heart.

"That is my affair. Now, Nadia," he said, and the creatures who brought her down already had hold of her arms. "Fare thee well."

Nadia tried to think of what she had to bargain with, but there was nothing. If she were to work for Lux in the upper world to save her life, she would have to cross her conscience—and indeed her soul.

Yet she felt that somehow the Great Heart was in control.

There was nothing she could do. She could offer herself and ask that she be payment for these hearts. It would mean Georgeonus and Holofernes would have a chance to make it out of the canyon. But she could not offer the Great Heart to this creature. It wasn't hers to give.

Or could she?

Since the Ruler Unseen was all powerful, ever present, nothing could really happen to the Heart. The Ruler Unseen could not be destroyed. She knew that this Heart could not be possessed by Lux. In an instant, she knew this, for the Heart swelled with its own love for him inside her. He who created the other. Yes—she must give Georgeonus and Holofernes that chance.

"Fine," said Nadia, "then do as you will. On one condition: that I truly am payment for the hearts. That they will exit the Nether regions safely with my companions." Nadia did not say *friends* because she did not want to show weakness.

"Done," replied Lux.

"Do I have your word?"

The creature's eyes narrowed and flared. A glow of embers ignited and stirred in his torso. But he calmed himself and looked through Nadia, the embers still burning, as if answering the Ruler Unseen directly.

"Yes."

Lux nodded to the attendants and then made a strange whistling sound. In an instant, a creature was at his side. The creature was smaller than Lux, but similar in appearance and larger than the other creatures she had encountered. Lux whispered to the creature, who quickly turned to look at Nadia and then sized up her frame. He had a military presence about him, and when he nodded respectfully to Lux with his hand on his sternum, he clicked his heels and turned to Nadia. She was struck with fear and knew that if she did not have the Great Heart she would have surely died from it. She supposed that no mortal dealt directly with this military creature, unless they themselves were of some importance—that it was he who gave orders to those lesser in command to carry out. He caused such dread and agony within her small self, but strangely the Great Heart looked at it with pity and love, and she witnessed all of this in an instant, astonished. The smaller creatures had to hold Nadia up, for her legs gave way, as the military general gestured to them, and they took her away, with him following behind.

She did not think it was possible, but she was brought further downward. Through cramped spaces and hewn-out tunnels and stairwells, she felt the agony of centuries of suffering crying out around her. Perhaps it was the Ruler Unseen which perceived regret, sorrow, and loneliness, for again her witnessing was accompanied by great compassion.

They ended at a round room. It was lit by a red glow in its center ceiling, and its edges were dark and obscured. There were glints here and there of metal in its hidden spaces: large objects of wood and metal and gear and chain, which she surmised to be torture devices. Another creature entered and the two who were in the room brought forth a table to the center. Nadia sensed that the creature who entered was someone from the upper world who had been sentenced here. He was human, and he wore a leather apron and a grey mask over his mouth, like a doctor. The general whispered to him extensively, and the doctor stared at the floor, not showing any reaction, or hiding it well from years of experience. Nadia sensed that he was a tortured man who had done some very bad things on earth. She realized then that the Great Heart was reading everyone down here, and nothing could escape its gaze. She saw that something truly horrible had happened to the doctor when he was a child on earth, and he became so damaged by it that he grew into a horrible, tortured adult. A swell of compassion rose in her, but Nadia was distracted. If she could read people, then surely she could discern what orders the general was carrying out upon her.

And then she knew. Of course. As the attendants put her up on and strapped her to the table, she realized they were going to try and take the Heart. Instinct and horror caused her to resist and struggle, and her eyes welled up with tears at thoughts that were a mix of her own and the Ruler Unseen's: that here was the end of her insignificant pathetic life—her young body was to be ripped open and cast aside like some useless, shucked shell, and she would never again see Georgeonus or Holofernes or Mabel or the Wizard nor find out about her family. At the same time, there was compassion again for these creatures who were so hardened, so sick, and so imprisoned in this dark wretched place that they could carry out such an act upon an innocent. It was too much, and the tears flowed, and her Heart was pierced and lashed by these offenses as it steadily witnessed the creatures with love. The doctor stood over her and was brought a tray of instruments. When he reached for a knife, she realized there was no anesthetic here, for blood and torture and the pain of ripping flesh, sinew, and bone was somehow a part of this culture; it was the backdrop that had become normal to these distorted, sick creatures—like music, sunlight, or the smell of baking bread might be to a well-adjusted household full of love.

As the blade was raised Nadia realized that the Witch and the Wizard had been watching her, and she could hear the Wizard chanting. In her mind's eye, she could see them in his workroom: a tower room that had a dark floor and walls and symbols and designs painted on surfaces with a silvery substance that now glowed. A bubbling cauldron stood on the floor, and the night bordered an opened ceiling, where heavy slate plates had been drawn back to expose the sky.

The words were strange, and Nadia could not understand them, but the Wizard held up his staff and commanded his voice toward the heavens, as Mabel, deep in a meditative gaze, controlled a shape forming over the cauldron. In unison they moved, and a glowing ball of smoke took shape which Mabel caused to rise by her hands. As the Wizard spoke, it shed smoke and became a glowing ball of light, and a ray shot from the sky into it. Nadia opened her eyes back in the room to see the blade coming down to her chest, but there was an ethereal globe surrounding her chest. She was surprised to see the knife penetrate the globe as it came down and the doctor sliced through her garment into her skin. But before Nadia could cry out in the pain, she felt there was an explosion of light, a blast, and a great force such as she had never known which pushed everything outward, including Nadia. She felt she was being torn asunder and no longer in her body and separated from the Great Heart. She was crying out, no longer hearing the Wizard's voice, flying through blinding white.

Of this Holofernes was certain. If he had not been there to knock some sense into Georgeonus, the mission would have failed. Georgeonus could not accept leaving Nadia, and when Holofernes pulled him back, Georgeonus lunged at him with a fury, not understanding how they could possibly leave her—heart or no hearts. Holofernes was much stronger, but Georgeonus' wrath made him a contender, and once Holofernes was sure the hearts were safely lain beside them in the cage, he boxed Georgeonus on the ears. Georgeonus struck back, and they exchanged several punches. Georgeonus' eyes glowed and dimmed, as the sapphire in Holofernes' sockets flared up momentarily, too.

"Don't shame her! Don't you see what she has done?" shouted Holofernes. Holofernes fully well understood what

Nadia had done, being in the military profession. Nadia had offered herself for the mission, and she had done so honorably so that the mission could continue—and continue it must. He knew that there were some things that were more important than an individual life: such as the lives of many individuals, or a goal or purpose for the greater good.

Georgeonus bent over to catch his breath, his hands on his knees, as he wiped some blood from his lip.

"She has honored *all* of us with her sacrifice. You should know that," he continued.

And Georgeonus did know that. But not Nadia. She was the one who had been sent to help him—the person who gave him hope in his young life. Her very presence brought hope to him, because it reminded him that the Ruler Unseen had not forgotten his family. *Not Nadia*, he thought, gripped with grief, feeling it invade his whole body like a dark figure enveloping him in its cloak. He swayed and was about to fall over when Holofernes caught him, stood him up, and slapped his chest a few times.

"She has honored us. Now we must honor her," said Holofernes.

Georgeonus stood at full height as Holofernes' words cut through the shadow of his grief.

Holofernes slapped him on the back a few times, lifted the cage, and they both nodded.

They began their ascent, and all the while Georgeonus' own heart said that he was abandoning Nadia, that he should not leave, that she would never survive in this place, that he would regret this decision, but he knew that this was not the time to listen to his heart, for it was filled with grief, and it would not lead him to the greater good. It was time to listen to the Ethos: what he had learned for so long in his tutoring. His mind would have to decide the ethics of the matter, and he would have to stay the course, no matter how difficult. All the while in their ascent, the shadow of grief continually pursued and threw its robe over him, weakening him, plunging his heart into the throes of anguish, but he kept repeating Holofernes' words to himself like a mantra, like a seed planted down in the canyon, which grew into a trunk as they progressed and gave him strength to continue.

We must honor her.

At first, they were prepared to fight the dogs and other undesirables when they reached the lower canyon floors. They were pursued by some agents of the underworld, but the creatures held back, following Georgeonus and Holofernes from a distance and watching them. This only worsened the blow for Georgeonus, for it affirmed Nadia's sacrifice—her payment for the hearts they carried. Indeed they were being let go, for two demon dogs chased them, caught up to them, and lay down on the canyon floor to transport them. Why they should be given such a courtesy, Holofernes could not understand, as he stared at Georgeonus in bewilderment. But Georgeonus guessed that what Nadia held within was determined to be very valuable, and something—or someone—wanted to assure itself of the exchange.

Suddenly the stolen hearts were of no value to it. But to Georgeonus and Holofernes, time was of the essence. They jumped onto the dogs and did not stop until they got to the ferry.

Nadia could only assume that she was dead. She did not feel her own eyes as closed, and when she thought of opening eyes, she could only see the white light. She did not remember enduring too much of the knife pain. It had penetrated her; it had cut deep into her flesh: the precision of a razor-sharp blade wielded by an expert hand. But it was like hitting a diamond-hard rock with a flimsy blade. Once it had come near to what it sought, the explosion happened.

Nadia did not think this was the work of the Witch and the Wizard, but of the Heart itself. No, Mabel and the Wizard had been up to something else with that globe. It was like Mabel's quilt that had protected her and the children from the falling boulders. Yes, Nadia had been somehow sucked into that protective globe, crafted by Mabel and the Wizard. Maybe so she would not feel any real pain—from the knife, from the explosion. Nadia couldn't discern the details.

There were footsteps. Someone was walking toward her. But she could not see or sense her body. They came closer and closer, until finally, they stopped. Nadia began to feel warmth. There was a warm sensation around her, and the light began to dissipate. And then, she could feel her body— at first warm and then bitter cold air. She was aware of being in her body, and she quickly opened her eyes. There was Mabel, staring down at her. They were in some canyon, and Nadia quickly sat up, shivering, and seeing that she was naked. Mabel had a white cloth draped over her arm, which she unfolded and wrapped Nadia in as Nadia stepped off the table-shaped rock near a wall of the canyon. The cloth was warm, and she clutched it around her.

"Mabel," said Nadia, "how did you get down here? Did Georgeonus and Holofernes make it? Are they okay?"

Mabel smiled patiently, helping Nadia to step away from the table.

"Oh, I suspect they're fine now" was her reply.

"But—"

"Come," she said, turning. She pulled her wand from her pocket, pointed it at the cloth, and the wrap sewed itself into pants and a belted tunic.

"But—"

"We cannot linger here," Mabel warned, turning to walk briskly.

Nadia caught up to her. "Aren't we in the canyon?"

"No, Nadia."

"Then where are we?"

"We are in the Otherworld. We mustn't linger!"

Nadia did not press the matter, but followed Mabel closely, striving to keep up. She had the feeling that they were neither in the underworld nor in a canyon. She remembered the ice castle constructed by the Voice. It seemed so long ago now. In that castle, when her thoughts perceived that perhaps it was not there at all, it would come into and out of view, disappearing before her. It was the same with this canyon. This time, she perceived her own illusion. When it faded, all she could see was light.

"Take my hand, Nadia!" said Mabel urgently, in a tone which alarmed her, and in a moment Nadia's hand found Mabel's, which clutched hers back. Mabel's other hand came around Nadia's waist and drew her close, and suddenly they were being sucked through some type of funnel. It was not comfortable; it felt dangerous, and there was great pressure all around penetrating Nadia's cells. Then they were travelling at great speed, and just when she thought they were to be completely crushed, everything stopped, and they were spat out of a rubbery tube, and they tumbled along a floor. The light abated, and they were in a round white room, much like the one in the Wizard's palace, which polished Nadia's suit.

When the room came into full view, Nadia saw the Wizard through a window soundlessly clapping his hands. He opened a door, still clapping, and Nadia stood as Mabel remained on the floor, clearly frazzled.

"Splendid! Splendid! And you didn't have to travel back through that *dreadful* place! Oh, I like that one, Mabel. I like that one a great deal. Thank goodness you're safe, thank goodness it worked, and you didn't get ripped apart," he said, patting Nadia's shoulder and then helping Mabel up.

"I think, Freddie, that our combined powers will need some work," she said, rubbing her neck.

"Agreed. But finely crafted and artfully done, I would say. Beautiful work, Mabel. Now: coffee!"

And it was as simple as that. They were back in the castle. It looked like a bright morning, and the Wizard was serving from a tall, silver pot hot percolating coffee in his study, blue skies around them.

They kept track of Georgeonus and Holofernes in one of the crystal balls. They were far along and would be back at the castle in no time. The Wizard, Mabel, and Nadia sat watching them, sipping coffee and looking out over the friendly clouds amidst the blue sky. It was all too strange to take in, for moments before Nadia was meeting death, or had met death. She was still getting her bearings, and no longer surrounded by that wretched place.

The Heart. Was it still within her? What had happened to it? Nadia looked inward.

It was there.

"Did I die?" she asked, her coffee on her lap, as the Wizard and Mabel heartily sipped theirs.

"What do you think, Nadia?" asked Mabel.

"I don't know. It seemed like I did," she answered. "But I still have the Heart. I didn't have my body for a time."

"Are you sure?" asked Mabel.

Nadia searched her face.

"You passed through the passage of death, but you were protected. You. Mabel," said the Wizard. He sipped his coffee and let out a deep sigh. "Ah. Magick is a wondrous thing."

He sprung up. "Oh—they are nearing the upper levels. We must go and meet them."

CHAPTER VIII
HEARTS RESTORED

In the canyon of Standhøfl Tourdemil, both approached the parents and children: Georgeonus and Holofernes from the west, and Nada, the Wizard and Mabel from the east. When Georgeonus looked up and saw a figure that looked like Nadia, he stopped in his tracks, for he thought that she was a ghost. As they got closer and closer, he saw that it *was* Nadia, and when they came face to face, he hugged her, looking then to Mabel and the Wizard.

The Wizard nodded to Mabel, as there was no time to lose, and Holofernes surrendered the cage of hearts. But how to identify whose heart belonged to whom?

The Silver Witch stepped forward. One by one she took the children gingerly by their shoulders and brought them forward. She raised her wand toward the case, and it enlarged. She waved it around, as if shopping at the supermarket for the right cereal. When she did, there was a flutter in the cage, and the heart that belonged to that child stirred to be reunited.

"Ah, there you are," she said.

Then the Silver Witch turned to the child and touched the girl's chest with her wand. The girl's arms spread apart.

Suddenly, they could see through her body the vessel-rich red cavity—empty where a heart should be—save for a grey stone. The stone began to vibrate, loosen, and when it disappeared there was a thud on the canyon floor. The child looked as though she could not breathe, and she let out quick gasps. The Silver Witch tapped the case, and the ready heart came to perch at the door. She drew a silvery line in the air from the heart to the girl's chest as the girl looked on, horrified.

Then the heart disappeared, and reappeared, beating within the cavity. The transparent window closed, and the girl's chest appeared normal, though the girl appeared to be in shock, still standing with her arms splayed. The Silver Witch took out her tin of silver goo and dipped her finger in it, and then she pointed it at the girl's chest. The goo appeared on the girl. As it absorbed, the girl seemed to come to, her arms lowered, and the Witch was already selecting the next child.

She rounded up the other children, taking their shoulders in her big, soft, gentle hands. The parents were fraught with worry, remembering that Magick was once a part of their history, but suspicious of what this all meant. In these circumstances, their only concern was for their child; they were desperate for their child's survival, and to counter this evil that had been done.

A question lingered in all as one by one the hearts were restored. How touched would the children be by this evil, and the memory of it? For how long? Afterward, the Wizard explained to the parents that the children would forever bear this mark. In some ways, it was up to them how much it would affect them. Desperate for more answers, and honored with the rarity of the Wizard's presence, the parents pressed him for more answers. But the Wizard knew that he could not interfere with the affairs of humans too much, or act as their counsel, so he reassured them, but knew he had to take his leave. None saw it happen, but before they knew it, he had disappeared.

Nadia bathed in the sweet, energizing, light-filled water and changed into fresh linens. Her body was tired, and she relished the soft bed and velvet spread which felt like rose petals. There would be a celebration tonight in the castle in the Land of Silence, with music. Some harps were rehearsing, which meant there was already sound in the land, for when music was played in the Land of Silence, there was sound, and people could communicate normally, or as they normally did here: telepathically.

There was a knock on the door.

Come in, she replied.

Georgeonus entered. He had removed the metal suit, probably for maintenance, and looked more human in the purple-magenta linen. His eyes were averted as he crossed the room toward the narrow, arched windows and looked out at the dusk. Nightfall was encroaching in the Land of Silence. They knew that something was wrong, for normally the nighttime of this bright land only reached twilight. Yet with each passing day, the dusk grew darker and darker.

It seemed unfair. Nadia was tired; she was tired of this problem getting bigger all the time. She wanted to be learning in school again, to spend time with Georgeonus. But school wasn't real anymore, and the things she had learned there did not teach her about the people and places that she had encountered, nor the evil that was spreading through the lands.

He returned to sit on the edge of the bed and continued to gaze outside. His back was broader, and his arms were stronger. Nadia crawled toward him and sat up behind him, her feet caressed by the rose petal spread.

His upper back seemed to bear a burden more than was seen. Georgeonus turned, staring at the bed. As if joining the conversation, Nadia stared at the same place. And then his outstretched hand was there. She looked up at him as he continued to stare at his palm. She was not surprised, really. She had known this was coming, known that it was why she had been placed here from the start, for a lifelong task. For a moment, her heart leapt. For a moment, she was able to feel the simple, ecstatic joy of the crush of love, coupled with the knowledge of their enduring friendship. As she placed her hand in his palm, she felt new feelings, and they thrilled her. Electricity moved between them through their hands. In the background of her heart, however, loomed the shadow of all that had been, of that large Heart that had come to dwell in her. There was something else, too. An ache that she could not define. As her heart swelled with joy, she felt pain: like barbed wire wrapped around the Great Heart.

She was relieved that this ordeal was over. She had been thrown into this world, but in the process learned that she was meant to come here. There was no going back to the old man and old woman on the farm. But where did she belong?

There was a quiet answer from the Great Heart within. It was not in her language, but it was a knowing that this ordeal was indeed not over. This answer loomed over the room, and Nadia felt a sense of dread amidst the courage of the Ruler Unseen. She was not used to the paradox of her heart against the Great Heart. It was like trying to grow into shoes the size of mountains. She could feel the way the Great Heart handled things: with courage, mercy, fortitude, and love, but her own, young heart was ill equipped to embody such strength, such maturity.

See you at the party, Nadia. Georgeonus squeezed Nadia's hand, rose, and exited the room.

After Nadia had dressed, there was another knock at her door.

Nadia.

It was Mabel.

Come in, said Nadia.

Mabel entered. She looked the same as she had in the Otherworld. Her hair was tied back, but some wisps were loose. She wore an apron, and Nadia imagined that there were all kinds of useful magickal items hidden in its pockets. She was not dressed for a party…or maybe she was. Yes, Nadia thought. She would go just as she was. It didn't matter what the Silver Witch was wearing. Her personality, goodness, and presence were such gifts.

I know why you're here, Mabel. Nadia wanted to save Mabel from any talk she felt she had to have. *I know that it is not finished yet—with Talmus.*

Well, she replied, *I see you wear that Heart well.*

I only worry for Georgeonus. He won't understand, she said. *And I don't either—not completely. It is starting to hurt, Mabel. To be around him. It hurts a lot.*

I know, said Mabel. *It will be best that you leave. But you will see him again one day. And you won't be alone in this.*

Why? Nadia perked up. *Are you coming with me?*

Mabel looked at her compassionately. *Not exactly,* she said.

Then where, Mabel? Where am I to go? she asked.

You will know soon enough. Now I will give you the coordinates to a door. You must go there and wait. Someone will meet you and take you to where you need to go.

Why does it hurt so much, since the Otherworld?

Mabel let out a sigh. *Because, I think, the weight of what is happening is weighing on the Ruler Unseen, and he is letting you glimpse that, Nadia, for whatever reason He has. And Georgeonus—you care a great deal about him. Your feelings are growing, and it just so happens that they are doing so in the Presence of this Great Heart. Oh, I don't think you'll have this gift forever. That's not to say you won't know the Great Heart; we all should. But right now, Nadia, he is dwelling within you like no other living creature—for a purpose.*

They were quiet.

Such sadness there, said Nadia. *How can I soothe the Heart of the Ruler Unseen?*

That's a big job. But in the meantime, I have something for you. The Silver Witch handed to Nadia a silver heart-shaped tin.

Nadia removed the heart-shaped top and peered inside at the sparkling, silvery goo.

It will only last so long, you know, not for the whole duration of your…undertaking, she continued, *but it will ease your suffering a bit. Whenever you need some relief, just dab a bit over your heart, and it will find its way in.*

Thank you, Mabel, said Nadia. She wrapped her arms around Mabel and gave her a big, long hug.

At the party, Nadia was relieved that Georgeonus had gone outside to skip rocks along the moat. The pain was getting progressively worse as the hours wore on, and being in his vicinity made it worse. The sadness that she was experiencing was like nothing she had encountered before, and it was challenging to put on a brave, smiling face for all the grateful parents at the party. It was a festive time, with a variety of music and instruments, food, and dancing. There were overflowing bowls of fruit, a variety of cheese plates and steaming casserole dishes carefully prepared, and desserts topped with colorful creams and berries. People were dressed in finery, and the sunset light streamed through the tall windows, bathing everything in a pink glow.

Nadia talked to many people at the party and learned that the Linen-Wearers had met with the Giants from Utsiket Sorghäven and discussed many ways in which they could work together to defeat Talmus. They agreed to network and reach out to outlying communities to discuss the dangers that Talmus had brought, and how they might guard against her rulership—through revolts. They rallied to travel to adjoining lands and spread the word about Talmus and what she had done.

But Nadia knew that Talmus had already successfully entered other realms. She knew it in the Great Heart. She was privy to much information there, and it was only affirmed by Lux's statement.

Do you think that these are the first ones to be taken?

In many ways, it was out of their hands. They had to appeal to higher councils, to the level on which these problems existed. The people were under the influence of spell work. But Nadia was glad that they were organizing and committing to being vigilant about what was happening, about what their rulers were doing. It could only help.

After Nadia had circulated around, and the party was winding down, she went to her room to pack. She felt that a great weight was upon her, and when she passed the mirror in the hallway, she was startled to see dark circles under her eyes. She felt that there was no time to lose, and since Mabel had given her coordinates and lent her a key, she would go to the Trees on the Hill—tonight.

She felt chilled, and when she got to her room, she found a suitcase in the wardrobe and a sackcloth cape in the closet.

With most of her things packed, Nadia walked over to the window to see if Georgeonus was outside. It was dusk—night for the Land of Silence—and getting late. She could not see him down below. She would wait until everyone in the castle was asleep. The music had ceased. All was silent again.

Nadia.

She heard Georgeonus once again outside her room.

Come in.

Georgeonus entered and eyed the suitcase on the bed.

You're leaving, he said.

Yes. Mabel—

I know.

How do you know?

She told me you have to go away.

Oh.

They stood in awkward silence.

I will be back, though, said Nadia, trying to conceal the pain, wishing she could leave now.

Well, then, said Georgeonus, advancing toward her.

He embraced Nadia in a hug, and she hugged him back, her eyes filling with tears. The idea of leaving Georgeonus made her heart swell with sadness and a longing for home. At the same time, being around him caused her heart pain in sinking, stabbing aches.

Georgeonus stepped back, turned, and walked out of the room.

When the castle was quiet, Nadia was ready. She draped the sackcloth over her head and fastened it under her chin. If she could just get out of the Land of Silence, she might find some relief from the growing pain.

As Nadia stole down the hall, she saw that Georgeonus' door was slightly open. She peeked inside, parting the door with timid fingers, hoping to get a glimpse of him peacefully sleeping. His metal suit lay on the floor, and he lay fitfully on top of the blankets in his magenta linen. Suddenly there was a lighted glow against the wall, from his eyes. He was awake.

Nadia turned silently to pull the door, hoping he did not hear her. But in no time, Georgeonus had stood and caught her hand, and when Nadia turned she saw his packed bag next to the metal suit.

I'm coming with you, he said.

Other books in the Evergreen Series

Christopher's Adventures in Evergreen
Return to Evergreen
The Rescue of Georgeonus
Nadia's Heart, Part One

ABOUT THE AUTHOR

Wendy Altshuler is a writer-producer who explores myth in new media. Her credits include award-winning screenwriting and WGA-accredited representation. With a degree in psychology and a Master of Arts from Columbia University, Altshuler documented the work of international choreographers, wrote and produced regional programming, and acted as a market consultant for artist-founded companies. She synthesizes her backgrounds in writing, production, and theatre to combine myth and media in a new way. She writes fantasy novels and creates works in stop-motion animation.